Diary of a Fairy Godmother

Diary
Fairy

of a
Godmother

ESMÉ RAJI CODELL

Illustrated by Drazen Kozjan

HYPERION BOOKS FOR CHILDREN ✴ New York

*

*

*

To Aniyah, my fairy goddaughter
To Russell, my prince
To my own triumphant triumverate of godmothers,
Betty Sitbon, Robin Robinson,
and Madame Maureen Breen
And to all who work hard to make wishes come true
—E. R. C.

For Alison
—D. K.

Earwax Moon, waning

Miss Fortune Harbinger felt it would be a good idea to discuss what we had planned after graduation, since it's just around the corner, thank badness. Mama says to cherish these years, that the first hundred just fly by, blah-blah-blah! I don't know what she's talking about. I feel like I've been in school forever and I don't really see the point of it; Auntie says if you're smart you can do without it and if you're dumb it doesn't help anyway. I can't wait to get out and start working. Some of my classmates plan to pursue further studies. Frantic Search is such a show-off and keeps going on about how she's going to get a degree in advanced studies at Hogwarts—as I said before, blah-blah-BLAH. Excuse me, we can't all afford Hogwarts; some of us have to work for a living.

Sinus Infection said she would like to get into agriculture, maybe grow vegetables that are so irresistible, humans will try to steal them, and then she'll ask them for their firstborn and stick them up in towers, or something like that. Miss Harbinger said it sounded like Sinus was really

1

thinking about things and then hit her with a peashooter. Miss Harbinger pointed out that tower-building is a popular option that we all might consider, and just because we're young women, we shouldn't think for an instant that we can't build a tower and stick somebody in it. Sinus looked pleased.

Twisted Ankle said she was going to continue to pursue a career as an artist. She is lucky enough to have a natural talent. In the back of the room hangs a likeness she rendered of a vampire bat that is so true to life that its eyes seem to follow us wherever we go. It bothers Belladonna so much that she wears a scarf to school every day, in case the image should fly off the canvas and bite her on the neck. Miss Harbinger clucked her tongue and said that art is a low-paying affliction for which there is no cure, and that Twisted Ankle was likely destined to starve alone in a cave full of those bats she likes so well, and we should all wish her good luck.

Acid Reflux plans to set up a clinic for animals, treating cats who have been wounded in broom-related accidents. Miss Harbinger advised Acid to study very hard, because it is even more difficult to become a veterinarian than it is to become a regular witch doctor, and you have to be well acquainted with the anatomy of all different species. Acid's face fell at the prospect of all that studying, and she whispered that maybe she would just go into taxidermy if it meant she could still work with animals. Miss Harbinger said an apprenticeship might be a good way to decide.

Velvet Underground said she was going to take over her mother's poison taffy apple stand, and Miss Harbinger commented that Velvet was very good at math and should have no problem giving the wrong change to all her customers.

My ears perked up a little, because I wouldn't mind running a business myself. My mother is a brewer, but I don't know if I will follow in her footsteps. Our cave is en route to the broom factory, and folks come by to pick up the homemade brews she's cooked up on their way to work. She has taken advantage of modern society; witches these days have so little time to cook for themselves. Still, I don't know how she can stand it, stirring for hours. It's a living, I guess, and she says it's good to work from home. Though what she knows about the outside world could possibly fit in a thimble.

I guess Miss Harbinger noticed, as teachers do, that I didn't want to be called on, and asked me what I thought I might attempt after I graduate. I said that I thought Velvet had a good idea, and I wouldn't mind selling something.

"What would you sell, Hunky?"

I admitted that I wasn't sure, and Miss Harbinger grew very excited. She said that sometimes the people who don't know what to do with their lives end up having the most interesting adventures of all. She told me to invest in a skateboard, the vehicle of choice for lost souls, and to be sure to document my current indecision in my diary.

Miss Harbinger encourages us to keep personal diaries for three reasons: one, in the event that we become famous, we can sell them; two, in the event that we become infamous, we can sell them for double; three, if we are good and bad, our diaries may someday even be admissible as evidence of our misdeeds in court and as entertainment for future generations.

But Miss Harbinger did not tell us what we are supposed to write that would interest a court or future generations or any other audience. So I am going to summarize what we read in class today. We were on chapter three of Venefica Mandrake's guide, *Be the One with the Wand*. The main idea of the chapter was "Eradication," or the getting rid of individuals who might cross us. The approaches ranged from the simple retort "Excuse me, you must have mistaken me for someone who cares" to the transmogrification of subjects into houseflies that can easily be swatted with one hand. Curses are addressed in a later chapter, Miss Harbinger says. I can't wait!

 # White Chocolate Moon, new

What a dull day. The sun was shining, so I stayed inside all morning reading cookbooks. There are some delicious booger cookies I would like to try, but Mama said to stick with the brews. If I keep making desserts, we'll be too heavy for our brooms to carry us. Do you think warlocks worry about such things?

Then we went to the supermarket, where Mama ran into some witch I didn't recognize but who sure remembered me. She went on and on about "Why look at you, dearie! Baddie me, don't you know I remember when the vulture first brought you, and now you're as big as a tumor!" As if it's news that I have grown in the hundred years since I was a baby!

Mama took the lead and went on about how I'm first in charm school and how "she'll be the wickedest witch wherever the four winds blow." Doesn't Mama know it's bad luck to brag? Well, they just went on and on and on, and there was the poison-mushroom pizza just defrosting in the cart and nobody seemed to care.

Then Mama dragged me around (in the sun, I might add) to all the cellar sales in the haunted houses so we could hunt for dolls for Mama's collection. Mama didn't have much luck at all. The good news is, I found a used skateboard. Maybe Twisted will paint one of her bats on it for me. Of course Mama had to literally talk the head off the poor ghost who asked, "Is that your daughter?" She read

6

that as a green light to go through her whole rigmarole again about my being the wickedest witch wherever the four winds blow—which, by the way, is Mama's fondest forecast. She whispers it in my ear each night as she tucks me in. Indeed, why wouldn't she believe it will someday come to pass? I am at the top of my class in charm school. I can make flowers droop like wet spaghetti! I can make thunder rumble like a whale's bellyache! I have cultivated a wart and a knobby finger, a taste for eye of newt, and a cantankerous cackle that rattles the bones of any vertebrate for miles around! And, as a true testament to my talent, I can turn any prince into a frog, yes, a frog—green and boggy and bumpy, with fly breath and slimy lips.

But I always change him back.

Mama says it's just natural rebellion. I don't know if it is or it isn't, but for historical record and future generations, I do think such actions disqualify me for title of wickedest.

"If it's so great to be wickedest witch wherever the four winds blow, why don't you be it?" I asked her when we were walking back to the cave.

"Hush your yap," she snapped. "I'm old. I don't have to do anything!"

"Well, don't you *want* to do something?"

7

"I *do* do something! I raise a spoiled brat who doesn't know the meaning of 'hush your yap.'"

Well, that's quite the career choice, isn't it? But Mama was only kidding; that isn't her real job. Mama was in the kitchen most of the afternoon, brewing something murky for the late shift to grab on their way home from work. She called me in to help, and I was crushing some herbs in the mortar, when she saw me and came running over, yelling, "No, like *this!*" and she grabbed the pestle to show me. Of course, I had no idea what she was talking about. It looked exactly the same to me both ways, and I don't care how she howls about it, I still don't believe there's any difference. I think she just gets a kick out of telling me I'm doing it wrong.

I try to be a helpful and faithful daughter. But I hope being the wickedest witch doesn't include stirring away my afternoons.

 White Chocolate Moon, waxing crescent

Miss Harbinger says I must stop writing in such a way that placates the teacher. Miss Harbinger says that means I must stop kissing up. Miss Harbinger says it is not necessary for a girl as talented as I to continually try to impress people with words like "transmogrification." Miss Harbinger says a real witch does not care so much what other people think. Miss Harbinger says that developing a personal voice in one's work is all one really can aspire to. Miss Harbinger says if I start one more sentence with "Miss Harbinger says," she will turn me into a dirty toothbrush.

Miss Harbinger wouldn't know half of what I do or say if Frantic Search were not such a huge tattletale. She would narc on me as soon as look at me.

For example, today was our spelling test, so Miss Harbinger sent word to a nearby kingdom that we were a group of princesses being held hostage by a ferocious dragon. It wasn't long before we could hear the thundering of hooves and snapping of branches as our rescuers approached. We hollered "help!" in our best falsettos, whereupon a prince, with such pronounced muscles that they dented his armor, flung himself against the door. Miss Harbinger opened it before his shoulder hit, so that he fell to the floor in such a clanktankerous fashion that it sounded like it was raining soup cans. His faithful men followed him, unsheathing their shining swords, but we wielded our wands at equal speed and turned their weapons into cattails. They looked very surprised.

"Where is the dragon?" the prince demanded.

"Disappointed, are you?" Miss Harbinger clucked her tongue. "Now, please behave. You are about to be educational."

"But you said that there would be princesses!" one of the knights began to whine.

"But you said that there would be princesses!" we chorused. (From chapter three, Be the One with the Wand: "Mimicry is basic to witches and all other brands of bullies.")

"Awww!" Miss Harbinger stuck out her lower lip. "They want princesses, girls!" So we waved our wands, and, in a rain of glitter, all of the knights, were outfitted in lovely gowns. Miss Harbinger took out her grade book.

"Belladonna? A little heavy on the rouge, don't you think? Keep it natural; I think a peach-to-orange would have suited him more, don't you agree? And Twisted Ankle! I said princess, not queen! Ease up on the golden tresses and double-check your work!" Twisted Ankle crossed her arms and grumbled something about having her creativity stifled.

The prince was unscathed, but not for long. "Now, today's spelling test is on class pets. The best spelling will decide what pet we will keep. Velvet Underground? Spell cat." Velvet promptly turned the prince into a very pretty Siamese, his crown slipping around his neck like a sparkling collar. "One blue eye, one green! Lovely! That's the Velvet touch!" Miss Harbinger encouraged her.

"Pffft!" Frantic blew a small raspberry. "Anyone can spell cat."

Velvet overheard and her face fell. I know Miss Harbinger gave her an easy one because spelling is not her strong suit. I think Frantic is beyond witchy to point it out.

"Belladonna? Spell mouse." Bella turned the prince from cat to rat. Miss Harbinger waited patiently while Bella shook her head and gave it another go, this time changing him into a sweet little white mouse with purple ears.

"Very good," said Miss Harbinger.

"Very good?" sneered Frantic under her breath. "She couldn't even turn a man into a mouse."

"Yes, she did!" I pinched her.

She pinched back, hard. "It took her two tries." Frantic tossed her black hair over one shoulder. "That's sad."

"Frantic?" Miss Harbinger called on her. "Spell . . . frog."

Within a moment, there was a textbook-perfect frog, wearing the unhappy grimace that only frogs—and princes that have been turned into frogs—can wear.

"There are five warts, Miss Harbinger," Frantic gushed.

"So I see. Very good, Miss Search."

I fanned my hand delicately over my mouth to disguise a smirk. My frogs generally have seven warts, but who's counting?

"Now, Hunky. Your turn. Let's make this a challenge. . . ."

"I've got one," I offered. I waved my wand and whammied the prince into a fabulous dragon, with emerald scales and a lovely fiery breath of three hundred fifty degrees (which, incidentally, is usually an effective temperature for baking cookies). In his surprise, the prince-dragon swung his tail and bashed out the back wall of our school, and all the knights in princess garb fell upon him out of sheer dragon-fighting instinct and beat him bravely with their cat-tails, following in pursuit as he fled into the forest.

"Well!" Miss Harbinger sighed. "I didn't know you could spell dragon! I guess our new class pet will have to be a teacher's pet: Hunky Dory!"

"Bleaaahhhh!" All the girls stuck their tongues out at me in tribute. I was very moved by their jealousy. We conjured up a new wall.

✶

After school I followed the trail of destruction left by my dragon until I found him curled up in a cave, looking glum, with his crown still hanging lopsided from a yellowing horn

13

on his head. He was panting smoky little pants, exhausted, and exponentially more unhappy than any frog. I climbed up onto an overhang and bopped him on his head with my wand so he was returned to his original princely form. After an amazed moment, he ran back through the woods, though he tumbled on something before making his escape. I assumed it was a tree root, but then out stepped Frantic Search in her designer curly-toed black boots, size fourteen.

"Were you following me?" I couldn't believe it.

"I saw you!" she accused me. "I saw you undo your charm!"

"So what? You must have me mistaken for someone who cares."

"Oh, you'll care all right, when I tell Miss Harbinger that you were kind and helpful."

"Really? Well, I heard that dung beetles don't tell tales." I raised my wand in a challenge.

"You can't do anything to me! We haven't learned curses yet!" She jeered. But I could see a nervous gulping movement in her throat, so I whirled my wand around a couple of times for good measure. She beat a hasty retreat, but called over her shoulder, "I've got more in my bag of tricks, Hunky Dory. You won't be teacher's pet forever!"

Teacher's pet? She really does have me mistaken for

someone who cares. I hadn't planned on being teacher's pet forever. Forever is such a long time to stay the same way. That's why I turned the dragon back into a prince. He was so happy, you'd think he expected to be a prince for the rest of his life. You'd think he'd never run into another witch or magic spell.

From chapter one, *Be the One with the Wand*: "Be open to changes."

White Chocolate Moon, first quarter

It is one thing to transmogrify, and quite another to bring things up out of thin air. I've devoted three days to the spell books (chapter six, *Be the One with the Wand*: "Where you devote your energy, so shall you improve"). Three days of teacups, hammers, hats, and sausages. Things we need but rarely wish for. Some things just appeared accidentally, and soon I was tripping over all sorts of clutter: cages and bicycles and clothes and platters.

It occurred to me to approach the task with some sort

of progression. Invoke a caterpillar, then a butterfly. A lock, then a key. An egg, then a chicken. A seed, then a flower. And then, by the light of the moon, I raised a beanstalk that uncoiled itself heavenward and disappeared beyond my sight. The feeling was electric. I climbed to the top, and, blissfully alone, I watched the moon hover above the roiling white sea of clouds. I used my force to grab falling stars from the sky and redirect their paths.

Did I only dream it?

White Chocolate Moon, full

Auntie Malice came for a visit. We were so excited to see each other that we bit and kicked each other and pulled each other's hair. I told her right away, "I hate when you come over, because your visits are always too short and I am always so sad when you leave."

"Terrible, isn't it?" She grinned. "I'll try to leave extra early, then, so I won't postpone the agony." Auntie is so thoughtful! Of course, Mama was beside herself with glee, and they set themselves right down to complaining. I prepared the ragweed tea. I was very careful to put the toe jam in a gourd, because Auntie has told me time and time again that one should allow one's guests to season their food to their own taste, so condiments must always go on the *side*. Auntie is a stickler for good manners.

I went in and threw the cup of tea at Auntie. Mama gave me a stern look, so I asked Auntie if she would like something with her tea, and she said yes, please, so I threw the gourd as well and hit her in the head. Auntie sighed and said if she were ever stupid enough to have a daughter, she'd want one exactly like me. Mama bragged about how well I am doing in charm school, and Auntie pulled Mama's eyelashes for bragging. Then said she knew a few kings and queens who could take some lessons. Auntie went on to bemoan how she wasn't even invited to the christening taking place at the castle today, and she's known the family for years.

"If I were you, I'd crash that party," I said, just to make a joke, but they both stopped talking and stared at me as if they were going to stomp my toes.

"Is she in the gifted class at school?" asked Auntie. "She really should be in the gifted class."

"She'll be the wickedest witch wherever the four winds

blow!" Mama beamed, and was promptly punched in the ear for bragging again. "Ouch! Let her come with you, Malice. She's been all cooped up in this cave."

"But there will be F.G.s," said Auntie, under her breath.

"What's an F.G.?" I asked. They glared at me and spoke in hushed tones.

"Bother! Well, she's got to find out someday." Mama set her hands on her hips. "Hopefully at her age she's beyond their sphere of influence." Auntie gave me a long look.

"What's an F.G.?" I repeated. Mama pinched me and told me to grab my hat and skateboard, and to mind my manners; Auntie was taking me to a grown-up party.

"Will you join us?"

"No, I think I will stay back and set rat traps. Why should this stupid cat have all the fun?" She gave Clot's black tail a yank, making him arch his back and show his pointed teeth. Mama giggled girlishly.

✶

"What's an F.G.?" I asked Auntie for the third time when we were in the air.

"A nincompoop," said Auntie.

I have not been alive very long, but I already have met a lot of nincompoops, and they come in all shapes and sizes and are hard to recognize by just looking; usually you have to talk with one for a while before you find out you are in the company of one. So Auntie's definition was not very helpful, but she did not seem in any sort of a mood to help me along. She was grumbling something about "EVery Other GAL in the PLACE gets an invite, and ME, how LONG have I KNOWN them, why, YEARS and YEARS, and my BADness, what kind of people ARE they, they probably won't even serve CHEESE. . . ."

Well, we soared and skated over the moat and the guards, and the porter at the door who was supposed to announce the guests conveniently lost consciousness when Auntie Malice asked him to check her boa and it hissed at him. Auntie asked me if I knew the way back, in case she had to make a quick exit, and I assured her that I did. As we entered the Great Hall, the jubilation of the scene that spread widely before me took my bad breath away. Even the walls seemed to be dancing, but it was just the flickering of candlelight. At one table a dozen women feasted from golden plates; their shrill laughter carried all around the hall like the rattling of cicadas. Some even had wings like butterflies, with a glittering dust that shook from them as they approached the king and queen and the bassinet in between. As each one of these beautiful creatures bent over the bassinet and spoke, a great roar of approval rose, and applause sprinkled like spring rain. The last woman walked away smiling, back to her golden plate, where the others gathered like sisters to kiss her. "Show-offs," I heard Auntie growl dangerously.

"Who are they?"

"F.G.s," said Auntie. "Fairy Godmothers." Her voice swelled with such disgust that I thought for a moment she said gagmothers. "Giving the infant princess everything the parents have registered for. Grace. Beauty. Virtue." Auntie clucked her tongue and narrowed her eyes, shaking her head back and forth very, very slowly. "Vapid little under-achievers, those F.G.s."

"How so?" I couldn't help asking. "Don't they have any powers?"

"They grant wishes."

"For a living?" Something inside of me plucked and sang like the string on a harp.

"I suppose so, but why, darling, *why*—" Auntie closed her eyes in exasperation. "—would anyone use their power to do *good*? The world is good in general! When you wake up, what do you hear? Birds singing! What do you see?

Flowers blooming! Little animals scurrying to their little animal burrows! Streams tripping merrily over stones! Cows mooing to be milked! And so on and so forth, all the way to the end of the day, when even the craters of the moon appear to be smiling down upon the wonders of the earth! Don't you see, darling, it's so terribly *trite*! It's been *done*! It's all one big *rerun*! There's nothing original *about it*!"

I nodded like I understood, but I wasn't sure I did. Auntie rolled her eyes and continued.

"Now, look, look, look at those girls!
Some measure attraction by 'oohs' and 'aahs,'
And how much you look like a flower.
But if I may offer you some aunt-i-ly advice:
Don't waste your time being flowerful;
Being smart is much more powerful!
What's more appealing than aptitude?
What's more resplendent than skill?
What's more captivating than competence?
Do you want to climb a mountain, will you settle for
  molehill?
What is more intriguing than intellect?
I hope that you won't swallow other swill;

21

It's true, trolls won't make passes
At witches who wear glasses,
But princes nearly almost always will.
No girl is more attractive
Than one who's interactive,
So plug in your adapter and
Live happily ever after.
Because beauty's in the form of a girl with a brainstorm!
I really mean it!
Beauty's in the form of power!"

Have I mentioned that Auntie has a degenerate love of musicals? Now and then she breaks into a number. I hope it's not genetic.

"Now, mischief . . ." Auntie's flinty eyes scanned the hall from corner to corner with an ember glow. "Mischief is original. Mischief is clever and creative and always *en vogue*. People sit up and take notice when there's a bit of mischief."

"But must all mischief be naughty mischief?" I asked.

"For your information, I believe the word's meaning comes from the Latin prefix *mis*, meaning naughty, and *chief*, meaning most important, or first. First comes

22

naughtiness, and first is best. It's right there in the *etymology*, dear. See, darling, you aren't the only one who went to school."

Inside, there were footmen carrying around little trays of pink squares, and upon stepping into the Great Hall we were offered one. It was a lovely little yellow cake with strawberry icing, and I asked, "What is it called?" The man bowed and said what sounded like *petee fwah*, so I said, "Excuse me?" and Auntie barked, "Petit four. It's French for 'too cheap to buy a real cake.'" The man frowned and bowed again to leave, but Auntie swiped half the tray before he could escape and shoved the cakes into my apron pocket. "There, now you have refreshments so you can watch the show. Now, go, go, go, darling, announce your Auntie to the royal fatheads." She draped her boa around my neck and primped it, then gave me a push toward the thrones. I got a lot of sideways glances, but managed to make it up the incline before I turned to the assembled party and pronounced, "Spiteful Malice!" I saw Auntie across the hall, energetically mouthing the word "the" to me as a reminder to present her as we have often rehearsed at home. "I mean, squirm, mere mortals! *The* Spiteful Malice, *doyenne* of the dark arts, has condescended to have an audience with you."

23

Auntie lifted her chin, and I must say she looked quite stunning in her purple satin dress with the high neck and tortoiseshell cape—tortoises sewn on at the hem, clawing helplessly as she dragged them along. Her red eye shadow brought out the black circles under her eyes, and the raven feathers on her head came to a neat widow's peak that accentuated her frowning brow. Auntie really knows how to dress for a party.

The crowd, buoyant with dancing and laughter and billowing gowns, at once parted and became silent as she crossed the room. Bouquets of pink peonies wilted at her passing and dropped brown petals with a hushed and crumpled breath. At the end of the hall, the king and queen cowered over their bundle, seized by a look of terror, as if one of the beasts from the forest was about to fall upon them. I could see the delight quiver in the corner of my auntie's mouth.

At last she stood before them. With a pronounced pivot of her hip, she jolted the bassinette out of the protective reach of he parents, then thrust out her knotted staff. "I KNEW you wouldn't serve cheese!" she howled. "You FOOLS!" I wondered if the king was controlling his bladder. "Weren't expecting me, eh? Did the invitation get lost in the mail? Forget to put a stamp on? Did you send it to an old address? Leave a message on my machine, did you? The dog ate it? Eh? Eh? Stop me when I come to the right one!"

"Forgive us," the king blubbered. "You see, we had only twelve golden place settings, and we didn't want to offend—"

"Didn't want to offend! Didn't want to offend!" Auntie singsonged. "A little late for that, wouldn't you say, crown-boy?"

"She is right, she was wronged!" one of the F.G.s stood and shouted.

"Wash all of our plates! Let Spiteful Malice eat off the golden plates!" Soon it echoed all around the hall. "Set a place for Spiteful Malice! Let Spiteful Malice eat!" I held my breath, wondering if Auntie would consider this reasonable.

She did not. Black smoke began to billow around her ankles, which is never a good sign. "Sit down, you overgrown moth!" she bellowed at the fairy. "Do you imagine that I am so easily placated? And anyway, why does everything always have to be about me? I am wounded yet again!" She lay the back side of her hand against her forehead. "Today is a happy occasion, the christening of your firstborn child. Come, let an old auntie see." Her gloved fingers moved delicately across the bunting like a black spider and peeled back the blankets. "Oh! She is a *dear*! Now, you allowed all of your *invited* guests to bestow a gift upon the newborn child, did you not? Certainly, you wouldn't begrudge *my* giving her a little gift, would you?" The parents looked uneasily at each other, and the F.G.s tittered among themselves, looking decidedly worried. "What is her name?"

"Aurora," the queen squeaked.

"*Aurora*," Auntie repeated with a sour smile. "Like the dawn. How original. I guess Tiffany and Britney were already taken, then?" She yawned and stretched extravagantly. "Now, let's see, *Aurora*. What gift shall I give you, dear. Hmmmm? How would you like to be good at playing piano without ever having a lesson in your life?"

"I-I'm afraid that gift has already been given," stammered the king. A small F.G. with an acorn beret waved tentatively.

"Oh? What a shame. Well, how about lustrous curly locks the color of solid gold, so bright that they outshine the sun?"

"Th-thank you," the queen quaked, "but once again,

your thoughtful gift has already been given." A tall fairy with lustrous curly locks the color of solid gold swayed her mane off her shoulders and waved. Auntie nodded in return.

"So Blondie beat me to the punch, did she? My, my, my." Auntie caught my eye and suppressed a smile. "Let's see. What to do, what to do! You already have so many gifts right now, sweet Aurora . . . oh, I know! Let me give you something you can open a little later!" She waved her hands around the baby, and a cloud arose that circled in a green vortex first slowly, and then faster. "When she is

fifteen years old, she will prick herself with the needle from a spinning wheel, and *kapow!* She will fall! Down! Dead!" The cloud enveloped the baby and then seemed to drain into the blankets with a noisy *whoosh.*

The crowd was aghast. It was as if the entire room had been engulfed in some terrible, sticky ash that suffocated all air and light. But no, the candlelight still flickered, the crystal still sparkled, and the black shadows danced and danced upon the walls.

"What's that? No 'thank you'? Did somebody already give that gift, too? Well, I'm afraid it's no trade-backs, no nothing-backs on that one. I seem to have lost the receipt, so you'll just have to live with it. Or, you can pass it on to someone else; I hear some ill-mannered people do that with gifts they don't want. Which reminds me: here is a gift for you, Mom and Dad!" Auntie reached into her cape and pulled out a heavy book with gilded edges and a title that read in elegant scroll:

Book of Etiquette

"I trust you don't have that already, do you?" Auntie bent over and kissed the baby, who promptly began to wail; it wasn't long before the whole court joined in.

"Okay, mission accomplished," said Auntie. "Let's go."

"But I haven't seen the baby," I complained.

Auntie rolled her eyes. "I'll wait by the door," she said. "My hanging around here spoils the *dénouement*."

People made way as I approached the baby in the bassinet. A small fairy, about my size, seemed to be guarding it while the parents wept, but she seemed less lovely than the other F.G.s due to her unusually large buck teeth. They made her look friendly despite her thin and pointed eyebrows. It occurred to me that maybe she didn't especially like having sticky-out teeth, but that they were, in fact, the thing that made her seem most approachable. I must have been staring, because she asked me, "Do you want to see me, or the baby?"

"Baby, please."

She lifted the coverlet and revealed a creature that looked very much like the pink petit four in my pocket. I had never seen anything so sweet and delicious and divine in all my life. Her tiny pearly fingers wiggled at me, her eyes moved all around, and her mouth was rounded in what seemed to be perpetual surprise. I couldn't help gasping.

"Doesn't her face looked like mashed potatoes?" asked the F.G. I ignored her, so she kept talking. "No, really.

Look! Mashed potatoes! If she spits up, it's like mashed potatoes with butter running down the sides."

"She does *not* look like mashed potatoes," I snarled in measured speech. "She is beautiful and perfect."

"Mmmmm," said the fairy. "You're not the one who has to be up all hours with her. Trust me, this kid's *definitely* not perfect."

"What was your *gift*?" I asked.

"Child-care services." Her nostrils fluttered as she suppressed a yawn. "Under my watchful eye until she's sixteen. Luckily, your friend gave me a break."

I didn't think that was very F.G. of her to say, but she smiled in such a good-humored way that I had to forgive her. "Hunky Dory," I introduced myself.

"Lemon Droppings." She held out her hand, and we shook. The baby started to cry again. "Wah-wah-wah yourself." She picked her up and rubbed her back until the baby let out a delicate burp and spilled something witchy out of her mouth all over the fairy's right shoulder. My heart did a flip. Surely my aunt did not really intend that the pukey little princess should prick her finger and *die*. Did she? Then again, the fruit doesn't fall far from the tree. Surely this child would eventually learn to take on the terrible habits of her parents. She would not send thank-you notes or hold doors open for people behind her and would start sentences with "get me a" instead of "may I please have." In fifteen years, she might become the sort of person who wouldn't invite me to a party. Auntie was right. She needed to suffer, if only to make her different from her terrible parents. But death?

A sudden inspiration hit me. "Can anyone give a gift to the new baby?"

"I guess so."

"I would like to give a gift!" I announced, and was surprised at the hush that fell over the crowd. "You were very rude to my auntie," I pointed out to the royalty assembled, "and you deserve to be punished. But there's really no need for the child to die. I'm sure my aunt was in a hurry and simply acted rashly. So, on the condition that you learn everything in the book Auntie gave you, forward and backward and upside down, and pass all you learn to your offspring, I will adjust the spell. When the princess turns fifteen"—my eyes slid toward Lemon Droppings—"she will fall into a hundred years' sleep, and so will you all, until the princess is awakened by love's first kiss or some reasonable facsimile."

Lemon Droppings smiled gratefully. "I could use the rest," she said. "Thanks for something to look forward to."

"You're welcome." The strangest feeling was coming over me, almost like a fever. I wondered if maybe the petit fours were going to come up the same way they went down, but no, it wasn't like that. It was a warm feeling, but it wasn't a sick feeling. It was spreading, though, from my feet and legs and into my hands and up my neck.

"You'll excuse me for saying so, but I never would have guessed you were a fairy godmother from your uniform."

"I am not a fairy godmother." I glowered, shaking my hands to get rid of the needles that seemed to be prickling from the inside. "I am a witch."

She shrugged. "Sorry." And went back to jostling the baby in her arms.

I almost asked if I could hold the baby, but I caught myself. "I am a witch," I said again, and Lemon Droppings gave me a look like *yeah, I heard you*, and turned away.

I am a witch, I said to myself as I fled the hall. *I am a witch. I am a witch.*

✳

Auntie hit me over the head with her staff. "What was *that* about? I knew exactly what I was doing! You completely undermined my power and showed absolutely no respect for authority! *Darling!*" She kissed me on the top of my head. "You are a witch, through and through."

I am a witch, I told myself. *I am a witch.* We started our vehicles.

"Did you see that one F.G.?" I asked. "By the baby? She said that Aurora looked like mashed potatoes."

"Mmm. Maybe that fairy godmother has a little witch in her," Auntie said absently. "You know, mashed potatoes are a very fine substitute for baby. Mashed potatoes with lots of butter and salt."

I was barely listening. I was trying to shake the fizzy feeling from my hands, and trying to drown out the question darting like a wasp in all the corners of my mind.

Can a witch have a little fairy godmother in her?

No. She can't. I am a witch. I am Hunky Dory. I will be the wickedest witch wherever the four winds blow.

"Did you notice how the smoke matched my dress? Inspired, wasn't it? Weren't they *wowed?* Did you hear what they were *saying?* They said I was terrible and cruel! They said they had never seen anything so dastardly in all their born days! They said I was a scourge and a curse upon the earth!"

"I'm glad you had such a good time, Auntie."

"Do you know what the funny part is? I wouldn't have even gone if they had invited me. Throwing a party because a baby is born, well, that is just *excessive*."

"Then why did you care at all?" I asked.

My aunt seemed quite taken aback. "Well, it's still nice to be invited," she said.

White Chocolate Moon, waning gibbous

I announced to Miss Harbinger that I'd thought I figured out what business I might go into. But when she turned and looked at me with her piercing emerald eyes and her straight black hair pulled back tight, I chickened out. "I think I would like to sell petit fours," I stammered.

Miss Harbinger turned pale. "Where in Hades would you have tasted a petit four?"

"Auntie took me to the castle to put a curse on a baby," I said.

She took a deep breath and the chartreuse color returned

to her cheeks. She laughed. "Of course. For a minute there, you sounded like an F.G."

The class laughed. "What's an F.G.?" asked Velvet.

Miss Harbinger ignored her. "But, Hunky, baking is more of a homemaking skill than a career. I mean that quite literally. A friend of mine built her whole house out of gingerbread, and lures little children inside and eats them up." The class murmured in admiration. It did sound like a very good plan.

"Does she lure babies?" I asked hopefully.

"Babies are very hard to lure," explained Miss Harbinger. "They usually can't crawl very far before their mommy or daddy scoops them up and wraps them tightly in their arms for safekeeping. Babies are considered very precious, and they can't be conjured up simply for snacking. If you need a baby in a recipe, substitute mashed potatoes. If for some reason you can't substitute, the best way to get a baby is to work out some sort of a deal before the baby is born. But be careful. Parents take babies terribly seriously. They are wishes that have been granted. Of course," laughed Miss Harbinger, "that's not our department."

The laughter of my classmates faded. All I could hear was my own voice inside my head.

I am a witch.
I am a witch.
And wishes are not my department.

O White Chocolate Moon, still waning gibbous

I asked Velvet why wishes aren't our department today while we were out gathering nightshade during recess. She said, we *can* grant wishes, we just don't.

And I said, "Why don't we?"

And she said, "Why would we?"

"I don't know," I said. Then I told her I knew what an F.G. was, and she leaned in close and I told her, *fairy godmother,* and she pulled my hair and said, "Who cares!"

I said, "Ask Miss Harbinger how to become one."

She said, "You're just trying to get me into trouble."

I said, "If you do, I'll pick all the nightshade and give you your share to turn in. You can have the whole afternoon to yourself." Velvet has to work all the time at the poison apple stand, so this got her. She ran off to gather newts. She has a thing for newts.

So in the afternoon, Velvet asked Miss Harbinger, "What is a fairy godmother and how do you become one?" Miss Harbinger threw a handy jar of old pickles at Velvet, who ducked and they smashed against the back wall. Then she said, "Good question, Velvet. Since you are nearing graduation, you might as well know, fairy godmothers are our unraveling. They use their magic to do things for others and they get satisfaction from doing it."

"What's 'satisfaction'?"

"Do you know the feeling you get, that starts from your feet and goes up your legs and into your arms, and your fingers feel prickly and the hair starts to stand up on the back of your neck and it's almost like a fever and you feel like you're going to be sick but you never want it to end? That's satisfaction."

"Like, when it's somebody's birthday and they have a lovely outdoor party planned and you release an angry boar that chases the children and eats all the cake?" asked show-off Frantic Search.

"Yes! That would be very satisfying."

Or when you grant a wish? I gulped. And I gulped again. I always gulp when I'm nervous.

"Besides," I said aloud, to stop my gulping. "There is

nothing original about doing good. The world doesn't need us to do good. The very fact that there could possibly be a wish in the midst of such perfection is the true evil."

"Answers like that are why you're at the head of the class," said Miss Harbinger, to make all the other girls angry and jealous of me and send me notes that say "teacher's pet." Miss Harbinger is a good teacher.

On my walk home, though, I wondered so hard that I tripped over tree roots three times. Is it really wrong to make wishes in the midst of such perfection? It is spoiled and obnoxious to want more for yourself. But what if you can design improvements for somebody else? What if you can rewrite somebody else's story? Isn't that creative? Isn't that power?

I am a witch, I said to myself. *I am a witch.*

When I got home I asked Mama if Auntie gave *me* a gift when I was born. She said she did. I asked, what was it?

"Curiosity killed the cat." Mama gave Clot a look that sent his back into a Halloween arch. "Are you sure you want to know?"

I decided to keep the cat instead.

White Chocolate Moon, last quarter

Witches and warlocks can go to school together, but Mama decided to send me to an all-witch school because she felt it would be easier for me to concentrate if there were fewer distractions. Mama clearly didn't realize that it's just as distracting to sit around wondering what it would be like to have some warlocks around. Velvet can hardly concentrate, thinking about the Opposite Hex. I know precious little about them; from what I gather, warlocks are a lot like us but few and far between, being so susceptible to black widow bites and often the test subjects of their wives' brews. Should a witch wife get cranky (which is to be expected), the poor soul is likely as not to be turned into a toad or a teapot, whichever proves more useful at the moment. For these reasons, witches and warlocks don't usually shack up.

"Like humans, the propagation of the population requires two," Miss Harbinger explained to us. "One to condemn the other with what is known as 'The One-Handed Jinx.' Originated by a witch named Agnezza while passing through the village of Humburg, this curse allows a subject for a prolonged stretch to only be able to work using one hand, while she uses the other to hold the baby. This is devastating, for as you know, the world of a witch is a working world. We are married to our work."

"What about love?" asked Velvet.

"What about love! Well, that's why we have cats, isn't it, for Hecate's sake!" Miss Harbinger huffed, impatient with Velvet's lack of common sense.

"Is marrying all that men are good for?"

"No, some of them actually work." Miss Harbinger pulled on her taproot of a chin thoughtfully. "You're right, you don't have enough exposure to men. Maybe we should have some guest speakers." Miss Harbinger does not like field trips ever since the unpleasant incident at the crocodile farm, but she is very big on guest speakers. Once we had some small people come: they were dressed to honor us and did a kind of work called "trick-or-treating." They were very friendly and excited to meet us. They had big bags of candy, which they shared. They explained how they had to work only one day a year, and that they had to string toilet paper all over trees on the properties of ungenerous people. It seemed like a very excellent and helpful job. I hoped the next presenters would be as inspiring.

Miss Harbinger conjured three figures, and we waited patiently for their perplexed expressions to wear off, as Miss Harbinger has taught us to do for guests. Then she introduced our class and invited them to speak about their present line of employment.

The first guest was a warlock, pale and lumpy and almost hairless except for a few threads poking out in a ring around his head. He wore a chalky black sports jacket with sleeves about four inches too short. "I am the Shadow-Maker, and here is what I do. A mother kisses a little child and puts out the light. Now, say there's a chair, maybe a blanket over it. I lay a little darkness here, a little shadow there, and look, oooooh! It looks just like a monster!" We stared at him. He swallowed. "So! Then the child screams, 'Mommy, Mommy,' and the mother is interrupted, and she comes in and switches on the light, and what's there? A chair, maybe with a blanket over it?"

"That's what you do?" Frantic scoffed. "Full time?"

The old man sighed and shuffled over to Miss Harbinger's desk. He arranged her ruler, a spell book, a stapler, and some pieces of chalk before stepping away from his sculpture, squinting, adjusting, and then stepping away again, to peer through a square he made with his fingers. Then he nodded at Miss Harbinger, who nodded back and shut out the lights.

A terrifying monster appeared at once on Miss Harbinger's desk.

"AAAAAAAAggggggghhhhhhh!" We all shrieked and scrambled for our wands and for cover.

Miss Harbinger switched the lights back on. Peeking out cautiously from under our desks, all we could see was the arrangement of school supplies. We broke into thunderous applause.

"He's an artist!" Twisted Ankle chirped.

The Shadowmaker nodded humbly. "I also can make cracks in the wall look like faces," he added shyly, "but I mostly just do that for fun."

The next man was easily recognizable as a devil, red from head to toe with slicked-back hair and a tasteful tie. "Take me, for example," he started out by saying.

"An example of what?" asked Velvet.

"An example of success, little lady! S-U-double-E-C-S! I had my sights set high even when I was a young scamp, why, not much older than you are today. I guess you could say I've always been 'red-hot'! Ha-ha! Started my own cottage industry, but one day my tail accidentally burned the cottage down." He held up his smoking tail in a gesture of exaggerated apology, but sprang right back. "But it takes more than a little accident to stop me, I'll tell you what! What's the saying? 'Satan never slams a door without setting a mousetrap?' Long story short, now I run a red-hot factory, yessir, I produce ten thousand bottles a day of barbecue sauce so hot and spicy that it'll wither down a townsperson's tongue like a piece of bacon in a red-hot frying pan! I underpay my workers and fritter away the investments of little old ladies on time-shares along the equator, and ask me what I drive, girls, just go ahead'n ask!" He waited while we all didn't ask. "Well,

43

sir, I drive a red convertible, girls, yessir, girls, it's red-hot! Maybe if your broom ever runs out of gas, I can give you a lift!" He pointed his smoking finger at us like a gun, smiled, winked, and made a clicking sound with his tongue against his teeth, which made us all wince.

Miss Harbinger didn't seem to know what to say after such a pitch. "Any questions?"

Belladonna raised her hand. "Yes. I was wondering. Do you think girls don't notice how many times you say 'red-hot'?"

Sinus didn't wait to be called on before asking her question. "Did you know my broom never runs out of gas? It always runs *red-hot.*" She pointed her finger at him like a gun, smiled, winked, and made a clicking sound with her tongue against her teeth.

"Smart girls, smart girls," he said through grinding molars, and from the pinched way he looked when he said it, it didn't seem like he thought a smart girl was a particularly good thing to be. "Tell you what I'm going to do. I'm going to offer you smart girls an exclusive, red-hot . . . I mean, a real good opportunity to learn what-all it means to be an entrepreneur. Any one of you who'd like to try and sell some of my good ol' down-home barbecue sauce, spicy or mild, I'll give you a deep discount on a case. It practically sells itself! In fact, Miss Harbinger, if your class would like to try to meet the goal of twenty cases as a class project, I can give you a special educator's discount. . . ."

"That's quite enough, thank you."

My hand shot up. "What's an entrepreneur?"

"It's a businessperson, Hunky Dory. A proprietor of a small business—" Her eyes slid over to our redheaded guest. "And one who starts her own business, from her own original idea."

"That's what I want to be!" I blurted.

The devil smacked his hands together, and then pointed at me so violently that I nearly fell off my stool. "See now! That's what I like to see! Step right up, folks, and take a gander at the little lady with a lion's share of ambition! What'd you say your name was? Hunky Dory? Well, there's a name that steps right up and says 'hello' if I ever heard one! I can see it all emblazoned on a corner office door, that's what I see, and you tell me if you can see it too! Now, Miss Hunky Dory, right here's my card, and right there's my name, Pete Huckster, and if you ever, ever . . . "

He started down the aisle, but Miss Harbinger blocked him with her wand and a steely smile. "Our next guest," she said pointedly, and up stepped our third presenter, a troll not much taller than myself with a nose like a shoe, a turned-up toe, and eyes as golden-green as coins at the bottom of a pond.

"My name is Rumpelstiltskin."

"That's quite a name." Miss Harbinger's eyebrows raised. "May I inquire as to the origin?"

"One part circus people, one part vampire, three parts vinegar," he replied.

"And how do you make your living, Mr. Stiltskin?"

"I can turn straw into gold."

We hummed our admiration generously. Precious metals are rudimentary for us witches, but pretty impressive for a troll. Especially such a handsome one. Especially a handsome one that didn't look all that much older than us.

"Ouch." Belladonna writhed, taking off one of her shoes under her desk.

"Yeah, I'll bet he puts the romance in necromancy," Twisted Ankle leaned forward to whisper.

If Miss Harbinger heard them, she ignored it. "Where did you study to do that?"

"I just kind of fell into it." He shrugged. "I dropped out of school."

We all leaned forward. If there's one thing more interesting than a boy, it's a bad boy.

"You can *do* that?" Velvet was shocked.

"*You* can't." Miss Harbinger raised her wand threaten-
ingly. "Mr. Stiltskin has a special gift, a *calling*, you might say."

"It's the only thing I'm good at." Rumpelstiltskin shrugged.

"You wouldn't know, since you dropped out," Miss
Harbinger chided him gently, "but there is something to be said
for focusing on a talent and pursuing it to its full potential."

"Oh, I plan to pursue it to its full potential." A smile
came over Rumpelstiltskin slowly, like the unwinding of a
snake, and when it was fully uncoiled, it left us all rattled. A
little thrill went through the rows as his eyes glinted yellow
at us, and his teeth seemed to grow sharper the more he
smiled. Even I felt a thrumming. He rubbed his hands
together. "I won't stop until I've infiltrated the castle."

"'The first step in accomplishing amazing things is setting
unrealistic goals,'" Miss Harbinger said, smiling. (*Be the
One with the Wand*, chapter ten.)

I don't know about that. Getting the attention of such a
handsome troll seems like it might be too unrealistic a goal
to accomplish, even for an entrepreneur who is destined to
be the wickedest witch wherever the four winds blow.

Lamppost Moon, waxing crescent

Another sunny day. There goes the weekend. What does Mother Nature have against us witches? I was reading *Be the One with the Wand*, but Mama soon put me to work dusting all of her collections. It is really getting impossible; she has so much bric-a-brac that I can barely turn around anymore without knocking over a jar of pickled squid or newt's eye. Then Goldilocks showed up, again, all sunburned and blond and horrible looking.

"Glenda Glinka has to visit Dingbat," she announced to my mother, and marched in like she owned the place.

I am not very fond of Goldilocks. I think she has very bad manners, and I don't know what goes on in her head that she thinks she can just walk into someone's house uninvited. Mama tells me to be patient; she's just a little kid and it's not her fault her parents are so permissive. I think people have been *too* patient with her, that's the problem. I don't know why Mama is so nice to her; she must feel bad because her parents never spank her. Or maybe Mama is just patient with anyone except me.

I don't blame Goldilocks for coming over to play dolls, though. We do have a pretty great collection. Auntie Malice started bringing me back dolls from all of her travels, so we have them from many nations, like Strega Nona from Italy, who comes with her own magic pasta pot; and Baba Yaga from Russia, with a deluxe play set that has her house on chicken legs and a fence of glow-in-the-dark bones. Then Mama just started collecting all sorts of witch dolls as a hobby. Witch fashion dolls, witch rag dolls, witchy figurines in shadow boxes. She finds a lot of them at cellar sales. She looks at their expressions, and if they seem like they have a little mischief in them, she'll bring them home. Dolls of famous witches from history are her favorites. She has an especially creepy doll from the Louisiana bayou, Marie Laveau, who comes with alligator shoes; Morgan LeFay has attachable feathered wings; and Joan of Arc from France, who is in a little tin suit of armor. Joan is not really a witch, but Auntie Malice says any woman with enough power ends up being called a witch, and after what that poor girl went through, she deserves an honorary membership.

Mama let Velvet and me play with all of the dolls when we were little, cutting off their hair and drawing on them with marker and changing all their clothes around. This sometimes pulled at the stitching because, frankly, Strega Nona has a very different figure from Marie Laveau. So Mama started making some of the dolls clothes, and then as they got older we had to be gentler, so most of the dolls ended up on shelves. To relax, Mama likes to set them up in little poses and scenes, stirring cauldrons or hiding behind bushes to jump out and scare trick-or-treaters on Halloween. Mama can be very creative.

Well, Goldilocks came over with her rag doll, Glenda Glinka, who was named after a famous witch who turned herself into a pretty little dark-haired girl and went to school. She likes to make Glenda Glinka have a tea party with all the other witch dolls. As soon as Goldilocks came over, Mama took out the grisly old box full of witch dolls that have already been given haircuts. Half of them don't even wear clothes, they are just all twisted in that box, but Goldilocks doesn't care, because, if you ask me, she is a little twisted herself. The first thing she does is pull off all their arms and legs and stick them in opposite holes. Even though I know they are only dolls, I wince. "There you go!" She pats one on the head after she mangles it worse than a ghost of a Civil War soldier. Then she plops herself down in the middle of the living room and makes all the dolls sit in a little circle. She likes one rag doll the best; one whose eyes are loose and missing nearly all of her yarn hair, and the stitching in her face is so worn that she has only a half-smile left that droops on one side. She calls her Dingbat and she makes Glenda Glinka and Dingbat talk to each other in strange little high-pitched voices.

"Hi, Glenda Glinka, how are you?"

"I'm fine, thank you, Dingbat, how are you?"

"Oh, I'm fine, sweetie pie, thanks for asking. Would you like some porridge?"

"What witch in her right mind eats porridge?" I looked up from my spell book.

"Everybody likes porridge," said Goldilocks.

"Now, eat your porridge."

"Oh, thank you, that is so nice of you. Yum, yum. It's not too hot or too cold, it's just right."

Goldilocks is completely fixated. I swear, she runs

through the same script every time she comes over.

"For Pete's sake, don't you know any other games?" I asked her. She stared at me blankly. "Like," my mind raced, "why don't you play doll parade. Line them all up and see how far they go."

"Or doll *beauty pageant* parade," she said, holding up a finger in a "eureka" moment. "Ah-haaaaaa."

"Sure, whatever," I said. "Just not the porridge and that awful please-thank-you-sweetie-pie business."

"Now, Glenda Glinka, you go first because you are the most beautifulest girl in the whole parade," she explained to the doll.

Did she actually say *beautifulest*? She has *got* to be doing that on purpose.

"Then, Dingbat, you go second because you are jealous and bad, bad, bad!" She whomped the rag doll's face down on the floor a few times. "Don't cry. You know you have to be second for punishment of being jealous. It's the only way you'll learn." She sighed. Then she shrieked, "Mama Witch! Which one is your favorite doll?"

"Mmmm . . . Heckedy Peg!" Mama called from the kitchen where she was working. Goldilocks dragged a chair underneath a shelf.

"Mama! Goldilocks is taking Heckedy Peg off of the shelf," I tattled.

"I need it for my parade!" she called.

After a pause Mama said, "Hunky Dory, get Heckedy Peg down and keep an eye on Goldilocks while she plays so that none of the parts go missing."

I was very annoyed. Heckedy Peg was a famous witch who came upon seven children, each named for a day of the week, and she turned them all into different foods for her dinner. The mother of the children saved them by solving a riddle that matched each child with each food, and then Heckedy Peg met with an untimely end (Auntie Malice says this is often the case with high-profile witches). Well, the Heckedy Peg play set had seven teeny-weeny little plates of food, which of course Goldilocks made me bring down.

"Next is your favorite," Goldilocks obliged.

"I like Befana." I went over to a different shelf and took down the doll from Italy. I like the doll's satin orange cloak and the overflowing bag of goodies that she carries. I also like the doll's face, all pursed and squinty and smiling, like she just heard a good joke.

"Befana's not a witch," said Goldilocks.

"Yes she is," I corrected her. "Befana was supposed to help the wise men deliver gifts. She got separated, and now she wanders around the world leaving gifts for all children, just in case one is the recipient that she originally intended. Befana the witch. From Italy. She's very famous."

"She might be famous and she might be from Italy, but she's not a witch." Goldilocks arranged Heckedy Peg's plates.

"Ma!" I called. "Is Befana a witch?"

"Befana is a witch!" she called back.

"See?" I said. Just for her edification.

But Goldilocks shook her head no so violently that her nasty little ringlets bobbed all over the place. "Befana helps people. She is a fairy godmother."

I could not look at her. I straightened Befana's cloak and turned her over to check for underwear.

Goldilocks was staring at me. "Are you *my* fairy godmother?" she asked. I ignored her. "Are you *my* fairy godmother?" she repeated, so I ignored her again because learning to take a hint, I feel, is an important life skill. "Are you . . . ?"

"I am a witch!" I exploded. "My mother is a witch and I am a witch, just like your mother is a . . ." I caught myself. "I am a witch," I repeated, calming down.

"Joan of Arc is next, but she's naked." Goldilocks held the doll out to me, apparently moving on.

I went into the closet and pulled out the box of doll clothes. "What should she wear? Bowling in Black? Breakfast in Sable? Night in Noir?" I laid out the little dresses. Goldilocks fished through the box distastefully.

"Bleah. These are all black." She nearly stuck out her tongue.

"Of course they are." I sighed. "They are for witches."

"Befana's cape is orange."

"Don't start that again. Wait, look, this shoe is kind of purple. . . ."

"Make Joan a pretty pink dress," she demanded.

"I cannot make Joan a pink dress," I informed her. "I do not have any pink fabric."

Goldilocks lifted her skirt rudely and exposed a pink tulle slip in pretty puckered layers. Now, I ask you, what is the point of being a witch if you can't put shears to a pink tulle slip in pretty puckered layers? In a moment I had cut off a big piece and we were at the sewing machine. I plucked a spider from the wall to thread it and we were off.

"Give me your hair ribbon," I said. Goldilocks didn't

55

argue, and rested her chin on my shoulder to watch while the machine hummed. I trimmed the collar with the blue satin to fall around the doll's shoulders, and then cut off another portion as a sash to match. I squeezed the doll through. Joan stared back at me, very solemn and elegant, now prepared to lead the French army *or* go to a cotillion, as the situation should chance to demand.

"Here." I handed the doll to Goldilocks.

And then it started happening again. That electric feeling that could frizz my hair. *I am a witch, I am a witch.* I tried to mash the feeling down with those words.

"Mama Witch!" called Goldilocks. "Hunky Dory made a dress for Joan!"

Mama came in, wiping her hands on a crusty dish towel. "Let's see," she said.

Goldilocks held up the doll.

"Do you have some kind of a flu?" was all Mama could say.

"I think, maybe," I gulped. She came over and felt my head.

"Hunky Dory is my fairy godmother." Goldilocks grinned a big toothless grin. "She granted my wish."

At least I didn't have to play with Goldilocks anymore.

Lamppost Moon, half full (feels half empty)

This morning Miss Harbinger wagged a piece of paper in the air and walked down our rows like a general. "Would anyone like to take responsibility for *this?*" She seemed to pause by my desk, but I had no idea what she was talking about, so of course I didn't say anything. She turned around when she reached her desk and frowned at us as if she were waiting for something.

"I got one, too," Frantic Search breathed. "I think it's just *terrible*, Miss Harbinger."

"One what?" I asked.

"A chain letter, Hunky Dory," she said, and then read aloud from the sheet she was holding: "'Make six copies of this letter and distribute to six friends within six hours, and your fondest wish shall come true.' Let's do the math. How many sets of six in a given twenty-four-hour day?"

"Four."

"So, if six wishes were granted for every six people who forwarded this letter within six hours in a twenty-four-hour period, how many wishes could potentially be granted in a given day?"

"One thousand two hundred ninety-six." How did Frantic know, off the bat like that? Velvet's the one who is good at math.

"Correct. More if they were fast. Someone must be very very interested in granting wishes. Who else received a letter like this?"

Everyone but me raised their hand. "It seems someone got hold of the class list and sent a chain letter to everyone except Hunky Dory. Don't you find that rather mysterious? Rather perplexing? Rather *confoundrilating*?"

I could not understand what she was getting at, but then it dawned on me: she thought I sent those letters! "I didn't send them!" I gasped. Frantic turned away, but not before I noticed her triumphant sneer.

"Take out your books!" Miss Harbinger snapped. A tendril fell from her black bun. "Open *Stunk and White, Elements of Style* to the appendix, Roman numeral MXLV!" She read aloud: "'Chain letters should be simple threats of an undisclosed nature to be perpetrated against the gullible and superstitious!' Miss Dory! Do you consider myself or your coven particularly gullible or superstitious?"

"No, ma'am, but—"

She continued reading. "Furthermore! 'Good form demands that a chain letter should not comprise of any misleading promises regarding future positive outcome should the recipient comply! Such inbreeding of dark and light magic creates a fever of annoyance and despair to which even witches have no immunity!' Now! *Be the One with the Wand*, page 332!" She thumped back the pages of her thick teacher's edition angrily. We followed. "Read and repeat! 'Live as though your fondest wish has already been granted!'"

"Live as though your fondest wish has already been granted," we repeated.

"Does anyone here need any wishes granted?"

"No, ma'am," we answered in unison.

"Not even by a fairy godmother?" She hovered over me.

This was too unfair. "Miss Harbinger!" I protested. "If it were I who sent those letters, when you asked who received one, wouldn't I have raised my hand immediately to throw you off the track?"

Miss Harbinger was taken aback by this and looked momentarily confused. She strode back to her desk and rubbed her chin. "Perhaps you didn't know, girls, so let me

59

offer you a first and last warning. Wishes can be very deep, dark things. They are too witchy even for most witches. Even for one with your talents, Frantic Search." She turned her green eyes on my nemesis, and then on me. "Or yours, Hunky Dory." A shadow fell across her face. "Wishes are the source of power for the powerless and need to be understood completely before they can be utilized in a witch's arsenal. If you know someone's desires, you can create the delusion that impossible or ridiculous things are within reach, and inspire great sacrifices. You can create a toxic cloud of dissatisfaction that will permeate every moment of your victim's day. You can turn your enemies against themselves, inviting destruction by their own rapacious cravings. You can go into advertising!

"Such is the potential of the wishes of mere mortals, so you can imagine, the wishes of witches have particularly great and devastating power." *Can wishes make things better? More interesting? More hopeful?* I thought. I bit my lip. Was this more of that rebellion that Mama was talking about? Why couldn't I just listen and accept what Miss Harbinger was telling us? "Toying with them is *grounds for expulsion.*" I could see Velvet looking worriedly at me out of the corner of her eye. "You have been warned. There is

entirely too much talk about wish-granting. I don't want
another word about it, do you hear?"

"But if we *should* have questions," Belladonna squeaked,
"is there a book?"

I thought it was a perfectly reasonable thing to ask, but
Miss Harbinger looked pinched and said, "No, there is not
a book." (In an unnecessarily sarcastic way, in my opinion.)
She sighed. "I guess the best thing to do is have a guest
speaker so that you can see for yourselves how undesirable
it all really is."

Hooray!!! FINally something USEful.

Miss Harbinger took me aside and said she was sorry,
but she was going to have to let my mother know what had
happened. I said, "You are going to tell her nothing, then?"
She said that the situation was too serious to try to make up
for it with a little extra-credit back talk. I was so embarrassed.

I looked at Frantic all morning with burning eyeballs, but
she didn't dare look back at me. "How far the fall from
grace," she managed to mutter in my ear as she left for the
day.

"Frantic did it," I confided in Velvet. "I just know it."

"Why don't you tell Miss Harbinger?"

"Because then Miss Harbinger will punish her, and then where's the fun for me? Someday I'll take the curl out of her boots for getting me into such trouble."

That's not a wish.

That's a promise.

Later

Luckily, Auntie Malice was there when Mama read the note from Miss Harbinger. "Ah, trouble in school! That takes me back!"

"This is serious, Spiteful. She was caught sending a wish-granting chain letter."

"I wasn't caught! I was framed!"

"And will you seek revenge upon she who has slandered your bad name?"

"With every dog-bitten bone in my body, I vow to use her own rapacious cravings as a map to her own destruction!"

"Still worried?" Auntie winked at my mother and sipped her tea. "Oh, sister, don't open your umbrella before it starts to rain. She'll still be the wickedest witch wherever the four winds blow, just as you say."

Mama still looked worried.

Lampost Moon, waxing gibbous

I decided to perform an experiment to see if Auntie Malice is right about there being only one kind of mischief. I disguised myself as an old crone by dressing in pauper's rags and scrunching up my face until it looked like a monkey's bottom. This is a classic witch's trick; the way people treat the elderly is a good gauge of what rewards—and what punishments—they deserve. I walked for quite a distance, and though it was a nice stroll, I didn't find anyone that I could whammy. I was surprised when I came across a shanty in a clearing deep in the woods. I would have guessed it was abandoned from the state of it, but the garden was arranged in tidy plots and some birds were worrying a full cob of dried corn hung from the porch. I noticed a well, so I knocked on the door, under the ruse that I might beg some water. When the door opened, the prettiest young woman was standing there. Her hair was in black, perfect coils. Her skin was the color of milkweed; it looked as soft, too. Her eyes were tired, rimmed with dark half-moons, but her lids framed two topaz jewels.

Before I could even ask for water, she cried, "Oh, you must be thirsty, old lady!" She was skinny and had bad posture, but she was quick on her feet. She skittered off and was back with a bent-up ladle. "You are thirsty, aren't you? It is such a hot day."

Although I was awfully impressed with her empathetic nature, I stayed in character, grabbing the ladle from her like a grouchy, impatient old harridan. I limped to the well. The girl skipped along behind me, smiling and whistling, like a sister included on some adventure.

"What are you so loopity-loo about?" I grunted. "You live in a shack and you probably don't have enough money for a crust of bread!"

"A shack is more than some people have, and while my stomach is empty, I can't complain. I can whistle like the birds in the trees; I have strong arms to work around my house; I have eyes that see sharp the soft clouds, and a nose to smell the gardenias . . ."

"And you're pretty," I added.

She blushed deeply, humbly, and looked down at her dirty feet. "Here I am, talking all about what I have. Let's get something for you! Dip your ladle and . . . and help yourself to whatever can be shared!" She spoke brightly and her eyes sparkled queerly. I peered into the well. In the little light that made its way down, I could see a murky puddle that barely covered the bottom, a miserable toad burping, and cobwebs all around the sides. I lifted my head and noticed that her garden plot was a yellow-brown mat, and the earth we were standing on was so parched it pulled away from itself into cracked, grassless pentagons. It was as I thought: the only water on that land was sparkling in her eyes.

I lowered the bucket and ladle into the well. "Pretty dry around here," I spat.

"Can't be lucky in everything," she said matter-of-factly.

"Live alone?"

"Yes."

"Any suitors?"

"Oh, no! Not many people pass through."

A real buried treasure, that one. I displayed my meanest grimace, but she just smiled back as if I had smiled first. Something had to be done.

I pulled up the bucket and pulled out the ladle, which turned to silver, studded with diamonds and a decorative hunk of lapis lazuli at the handle. I was feeling creative.

"Oh!" The girl did a double take.

I dipped the ladle in the bucket and said, "Drink your fill once," filling the ladle with water and a goldfish. I sipped it noisily. I lowered the bucket into the well again, brought it up and said, "Drink your fill twice," filling the ladle with milk. When I said, "Drink your fill thrice," the ladle dribbled over with pink lemonade with big hunks of fruit bobbing in it, and a little ice cream mixed in. The girl stood there, her mouth hung open like a door off of its hinge.

For the finale, I said, "Drink your fill *nice*," and brought up a shiny, naked baby in the bucket, cooing, with arms outstretched for her new mama. It was all I could do to keep from hopping around and shouting "I did it!"

I handed the baby and the ladle to the awestruck girl and started to walk away. "Don't forget to sing it lullabies," I added thoughtfully, taking off my costume as I walked.

"But . . ."

"Don't forget to sing it *lullabies*," I repeated.

She looked blank for a moment while the child pulled

playfully on her perfect curls. Then she opened her mouth and sang:

> "My sweet little honeybee,
> Sweet as the honey in the honey tree . . ."

From her lips poured rubies, gold coins, emeralds, pearls, sapphires, you know, all like that. She started to cry tears of joy, which turned into opals as they rolled down her cheeks.

"Thank you! Thank you!" She could barely breathe.

"Don't mention it." I waved. Even when I was a ways off in the forest, I could hear her sing, "Drink your fill twice, my baby-so-nice," and the clinking of jewels as they poured from her mouth. The delighted squeals of her baby made me laugh to myself. Wasn't that baby cute! Wasn't that lady beautiful! I was thinking that some prince will discover her, now that she has money.

"Yay!" came a voice. The F.G. I'd met at Aurora's christening stepped out from behind a rock, applauding. Can't I do anything without someone sneaking up on me? "Bravo! Girl, you completely beat me to the punch! Hunky Dory, isn't it? Remember me, Lemon Droppings? Wow! Well

done! That was brilliant! I knew you were in the sisterhood the moment I saw you!"

"Then you don't know much." I pushed past her. "I didn't grant any wishes. She didn't ask for anything."

"Oh, don't be so modest! You figured out what she wanted without her even having to ask! That's the hardest! Wait! Where are you going?"

"Home. To my cave and my cauldron and my skateboard.

I'm a witch, Lemon Droppings, like I told you before. That was just an experiment."

"Some experiment! You handled it like a real pro! Where did you learn?"

I shrugged. "Just studied some spell books."

"You witches are such do-it-yourselfers! Wow!"

I had never thought of it that way.

"Hey, do you have a witch's hat? I always wanted to try on a witch's hat."

"I usually just wear a bandanna," I explained. "Don't believe the hype."

"Oh, well. I'll let you try on my wings, if you want."

"They come off?"

"Sure. They're just jewelry." She smiled with her big teeth. "Don't believe the hype." She slipped them off around her arms and held them out to me.

"That's okay." I stepped back. Was she crazy? What if someone should see?

"Oh. Well, do you want to come by the castle sometime?"

I didn't dare consider it. "I've got to go," I said, trying to be rude.

"If you ever change your mind, wow, that'd be great! I'm bored out of my skull. Nothing but babies and those disgusting petit fours to eat. I mean, not that you'd eat babies. Ha-ha! Who would eat a baby?" She looked thoughtful for a moment. Then she looked *hungry* for a moment.

"Nobody," I reminded her.

"Of course." She smiled in an obligatory way.

The rest of the walk, I felt like I was floating. *Do you know the feeling you get, that starts from your feet and goes up your legs and into your arms, and your fingers feel prickly and the hair starts to stand up on the back of your neck and it's almost like a fever and you feel like you're going to be sick but you never want it to end?* A real F.G. said wow! Good job! *Who cares?* A part of me chided. But another part of me answered, *I do.*

The thought that I might know something that Miss Harbinger doesn't know, that Mama and maybe even Auntie Malice doesn't know, has me shaken.

Lamppost Moon, full

I intercepted Velvet getting ready to leave the poison apple stand. "Come on," I commanded. "It's something important."

She wiped her hands and began changing her apron, hurrying to join me. "Where are we going?"

"To grant wishes." She stopped in her tracks and looked wide-eyed at me, as if she did not dare to take another step. "I didn't send those letters," I insisted.

"I know, but . . . people are talking, Hunky."

"If people are talking already, there's nothing to lose, is there? I've got to try. The thought of it is sticking me like a bramble. What could it hurt to try?"

Velvet looked uncomfortable, but she called over her shoulder, "Ma, I'm going . . ."

". . . to help Hunky with her homework," I hissed.

". . . to help Hunky with her homework." She scowled at me.

"It's not really a lie," I whispered weakly. Still scowling, she followed me into the woods.

"Come on, let's get it out of your system," she grumbled. It didn't take me long to regret dragging Velvet along. It is nearly impossible to find someone who doesn't run away when they see one witch coming, let alone two. After we had the fifth door slammed in our faces, I wanted to suggest that we disguise ourselves, but Velvet already seemed awfully put out by the whole excursion so I didn't dare. Finally, I was able to give a young woodsman a mustache, and Velvet gave a fly to a spider. Altogether, not very successful by my estimation. The woodsman felt handsomer in his mustache, but it didn't actually suit him. So does that count? As for the spider's wish, I don't think it was very nice for the fly. Besides, the spider didn't really need her, did he? The thought crossed my mind that actually a lot of wishes can be granted without much magic, but I shook it off.

"Maybe we should give it a rest." Velvet was sweating and tired. "Granting wishes is a drag. It involves too much walking and talking and caring about people. Honestly, I can't think of anything less satisfying."

"Well, you were a good friend, to come along," I offered weakly.

"If you were a real friend, you wouldn't have asked me. I can't believe I granted a wish, even an eensy-weensy spider one."

"That was hardly a wish at all, Velvet, you shouldn't feel too goodly. And if anyone should bring it up . . ."

She rolled her eyes and flopped down on some moss. "If anyone should bring it up, I'll pretend I don't even know your name."

I was trying to hide my disappointment that the wonderful

72

fizzy feeling had not returned. Not to mention my worry about how long it would take for Velvet to stop being angry with me.

"Maybe we were rushing," I suggested. "Maybe . . ." Velvet was snoring less than delicately. Now what was I supposed to do? I wanted to keep practicing wishcraft, but I was afraid to leave her out alone, asleep in the open where the wolves or wand-snatching trolls might come upon her. I sat brooding, tapping my wand on my knee and watching it spark, anxious to continue our work. Impulsively, using my wand like a pen, I drew up a window in the middle of the forest to look out of while Velvet slept, and chanted:

"Do you know the kind of dream
That you grasp at the edges when daylight breaks?
Do you know the kind of dream
That feels as deep as a thousand lakes?
Give her that dream, the kind of dream
That you never want to end.
Make the impossible come to life
For my dear and wicked friend!"

The shutters flew open and a skein of fabric that looked like the night sky, alive with glittering stars, unraveled itself and spread like a slow-falling parachute around her. I could watch her dream through the window: Velvet's hair, twice as long and black, grew and fell to her feet before my eyes. Adorned in an armor of emerald scales and talonlike white fingertips with a matching bony crown, she looked quite fearsome and beautiful at once, wielding a scepter topped with a poison apple. Who dared approach this mighty queen? Oh, a Chameleon Prince, who wound his graceful tail around her and unsheathed his sword, lifting it high in her honor before slashing the hands off of a clock. Lightning flashed and clouds roiled in every corner of the sky. On rows of shelves behind them, jars full of newts in every color and pattern swam in joyful circles at the prospect of their union. Witches and alligators spun around them in concentric circles, big ones and little ones, the witches turning somersaults in their triangular hats, cheering and banging on cauldrons. The scene was as dizzying to watch as the turning of a kaleidoscope. When I turned away, there was Velvet, cackling in her sleep beneath the blanket of her perfect dream. *I want to grant wishes!* I whispered into my hand, so the trees wouldn't hear. The wonderful feeling frothed up in me again, and I basked in the selfish relief of generosity's spell. Like a dream, I didn't want it to end. But even Velvet's prince, for

all the boldness of his blade, could not rescue us from the passing hours, and time delivered us heavily to the inevitable awakening of who we are, and who we have to be.

✳

When Mama came in to say good night, my mischief was troubling me, so I asked her, what kind of magic is dreaming?

"Dreams are the great equalizer," Mama explained. "They are what make a poor man a king and a rich man a pauper, if only for the night."

"So, they are wishes?"

"I've got to wash the cauldrons," Mama said.

Lamppost Moon, last quarter

Miss Harbinger said we could make "Just Say No to F.G.s" posters to decorate for our guest, and, I don't know, I thought that was kind of rude, so I just drew a big pink petit four so there wouldn't be room for the words. I got yelled at for having a pink crayon, and Miss Harbinger

76

crumpled the whole thing up and threw it in the garbage can. So I did it over in purple, but I just don't think it looked as good.

Miss Harbinger has been in a very bad mood lately. I told Mama and she said, "Just see that you don't do anything to raise her ire." I said, "What's an ire?" And she said, "It's a thing you don't raise, you smart aleck."

 # Lamppost Moon, waning crescent

I was excited about the guest speaker, but guess what? In stepped Lemon Droppings. I slunk down in my seat and reached for my wand so that I could turn invisible, but it wasn't sharpened so I said, "Frantic, lend me your wand!" She stuck her nose in the air and said no, and Velvet started passing me one, but it was too late because Lemon Droppings was already jumping up and down and waving at me and calling, "Hi, Hunky Dory!" from the front of the room!

I pretended like I didn't see her but she didn't give up.

She called out, "Hunky, it's me, Lemon Droppings!" And I looked at her like, of course it's you, who else would it be? And Miss Harbinger asked Lemon Droppings, "You know her?" and she answered, "We're friends!" And Miss Harbinger said, "Is this true?"

And I almost said no, no way, but then I looked at Lemon Droppings standing all alone in her stupid pink dress with butterflies and tulips and her stupid buck teeth in a cave full of stupid, stupid, stupid witches, including Frantic Search, who wouldn't even lend me her stupid wand, and I said, "Yes!" Miss Harbinger looked as mad as I've ever seen her and she walked right over to me and grabbed me by the ear and dragged me out.

When we were outside she started yelling at me, "So it was you who sent the chain letter!"

"I did not!" I stomped.

"Oh, Hunky! I'm proud of you for lying, but who else could it be? I'm so disappointed in you. I would never have expected that you of all witches would be cavorting with such tyrannical saboteurs! You, who could have been the wickedest witch wherever the four winds blow!"

I winced. I shook her off and told her that I never had a chance to cavort, and I reminded her that she wasn't my mother. "And do you know what else? I think you are racist against fairy godmothers!" Even I could not believe I'd said it.

She turned so white she was nearly silver, and little static flashes of lightning crackled at the roots of her hair. She said she might not be my mother but she plans to talk to her, and that I am not welcome in her class until she does. The worst part is that I didn't get to hear what Lemon Droppings had to say.

✴

I waited behind a rock until Velvet passed so I could ask her what happened. Velvet told me, "That girl barely got to say anything. Most of the time was spent pulling her hair and pinching her until she got fed up and bit Frantic with her wonky teeth and then everyone cheered. Then Miss Harbinger got mad and said it was all your fault."

"*My* fault! I wasn't even in the room!"

"She said if you hadn't kept bothering her about the topic she never would have pursued it for our edification. She said you are a corrupting force, even for witches. I don't know how you can go back there, Hunky. You're in an awful lot of trouble."

I didn't mean to be a . . . disappointment. I guess deep

down I knew I could never be the witch they wanted me to be.

"Don't drop out," Velvet begged. "If you do, Frantic Search will be at the head of the class."

"I can't help it. It's who I am. I'm not trying to be one thing or another. I'm just trying to be myself. And it turns out what I am is different from everybody else." I felt myself gulping so hard that for a moment, all I could do was shrug. "I don't want to choose, I don't want a label, I don't want a reason for people not to be my friend. But I can't pretend not to know what I know. And I can't pretend it isn't important."

Velvet stood there with her mouth agape, and then she closed it and bit her lip. "Well, if you are going to leave us to be an F.G.—" She looked at me straight in the eye. "Don't just be any F.G. Be the best one. The one everyone will talk about for years."

I smiled at Velvet and told her to open her hand. When she did, there was a green newt in it. She pulled off the newt's tail and handed it to me as a symbol of her loyalty. Then she burst out crying and ran home without even looking back.

Velvet is a big baby. It made me cry, too, thinking what a big baby she is. Not the pink petit-four kind, either.

Lamppost Moon, still waning crescent

I asked Mama as casually as I could over breakfast what she would think if I just took a little time off to try to figure things out. I couldn't see her face, her back was to me and she was stirring some potion, as usual, but I could see she'd stopped stirring.

"What things?" she asked the pot.

"Oh, things," I twittered. "Career choices."

"There are no career choices."

"That's not true. Miss Harbinger says we can run businesses. We can build towers. We can grow flowers."

"Witches can do all those things! So you're a witch. There's your career. The end."

"Well, what about fairy godmothering?"

"Yes, what about it?"

"They grant wishes. And Miss Harbinger says that that is some of the most powerful—"

"Miss Harbinger says! Miss Harbinger says! Well, you'd better give a listen to what Mama says! You are a witch, Hunky Dory. And little witch girls who know better than their own mothers what is best are going to have to learn the hard way." Then she started stirring again.

She didn't look at me for the rest of breakfast, and I could feel every swallow of cold cereal drop down my throat like a ball bearing into my stomach.

I went on to school. "Where is your mother?" Miss Harbinger asked at the door.

"I don't see how my problems are any of her business," I explained. "I have only come back for my copy of *Be the One with the Wand*, which I believe my fees have paid for." I explained that I would not be staying, as I wanted to pursue wishcraft rather than witchcraft for a while. Miss Harbinger told me if I would write "I will not do any sappy such thing!" five thousand times, all would be forgiven, because she knew deep down I was a stubborn, arrogant brat, and have proven myself to be belligerent as well. But I refused.

"'Praise is no substitute for achievement,'" I quoted. "*Be the One with the Wand*, chapter seven.*"

"Fine," she said. "As of this moment, you are expelled. Go in and collect your things." I had to laugh to myself a little bit, realizing that Miss Harbinger had granted my wish.

Almost all of my classmates were very sad, and waved

their tongues at me as a farewell. I waved back. I was in a daze. I knew Miss Harbinger would be angry, or sorry or sad, but really! I never thought she'd be so unreasonable.

When I hid my diary and my textbook in a tree, I could hear the whispers. The trees tattled with every splinter of their timber. "Wisshhhhes."

"Whooo?" asked the owls.

"Hunky Dorrrry. Hunky Dorrrry," croaked the frogs.

"Oh, get a life!" I yelled. I didn't hear them pass *that* along.

When I got home, Mama had already heard the gossip in the air. "I should have known as soon as you made that pink dress for Goldilocks that something was off."

"Nothing is off," I said. "I am trying something new, that's all." This did not go over well. She beat me soundly with a broomstick and kicked me out of the cave. "Why are you behaving like this?" I demanded.

"This is called tough love!" It looked a lot like a temper tantrum to me. "And don't go running to your Auntie Malice, either! I could rip her nose hairs out! I hold her completely partially responsible!" I simply sighed as she threw out my skateboard, my cauldron, my cookbooks, and for a final indignity, my cat, Clot. He hissed at me and marched right back into the cave. Mama let him in. "At least *some* people around here have sense enough to appreciate a bad thing," she snarled.

She waited for me to come back at her with a nasty retort, something to bring us together again. I chose not to. That's when her eyes went wet, and her chin began to tremble. She turned away, slamming the cave door behind her. I gathered my things in the cauldron.

So that's the end of that. Here am I, hardly a hundred years old, and off on my own! I suppose it is for the best, and someday the rest of them will know it. I know I am not supposed to open my umbrella until it starts to rain, but now seems like as good a time as any, as it is coming down, with thunder and lightning, and I am lost in a dark forest. Ta-ta!

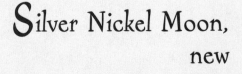

Silver Nickel Moon, new

I figured out where to live!

I guessed that none of my coven could take me in; I have

likely been branded a good influence. I didn't want to go to Aunt Malice; there only would have been a scene if Mama found me there. Then I remembered there was someone who owed me a favor, and after some effort I was able to relocate the house where I drew the baby out of the well.

I don't know why I was expecting the lady of the house to still be there, after making her so rich. Once she could afford a better location, why would she live in the boonies? This time, the property looked truly abandoned: the shanty was near collapse, and the garden overrun with rabbits. I determined to make it my own.

After decimating the hovel with a small whirlwind, I conjured up some chocolate-chip cookie dough and rebuilt. I never did care too much for gingerbread. I don't plan on eating any children—fattening, and I'm rather plump as it is. The new place is cozy and it smells good, too. I turned the rabbits into worms, and they are busy turning the soil. I'll have the garden back in no time.

Silver Nickel Moon, waxing crescent

I had a productive day today. I gave a woodcutter an ax that was always sharp, and a heads-up about the lady who sings 24-karat lullabies. . . . Maybe he can get to her before the princes do. I also granted a poet a pen that never runs out of ink. It's such a pleasure to come across sensible people. Hansel and Gretel stopped by, looking for the gingerbread house. I let them nibble on my doorknob and window shutter to tide them over. They said they liked chocolate chip better anyway, tee-hee! Gave them some magic bread crumbs that birds don't eat. They said thank you—nice manners, those kids.

Silver Nickel Moon, first quarter

Now, who should I have caught stealing a pie off my windowsill but Rumpelstiltskin!

"Hey, aren't you that girl with the funny name from the charm school?"

He's should talk. Having dropped out of charm school himself, he isn't one to judge. Still, I was so happy to see him. We had a cheerful afternoon. It was nice to throw a teacup at someone and we talked like old friends. He took care not to ask me a single thing about myself or my situation. Wasn't that considerate of him? Having been in the same boat, I imagine he was trying not to bring up old wounds. Instead, he regaled me with his own misadventure: he'd met some girl who'd been kidnapped by a king; some sort of misunderstanding about the girl being able to turn straw into gold. Honestly!

"Turns out he'll have her head on a platter if she doesn't come through. Pretty desperate situation." He leaned back in his chair. "So I tried to think of a price for my services. What do you charge, by the way?"

I hadn't been charging anything, but I didn't want to sound ignorant, so I said, "One gold coin."

"You're cheap!" He choked on his tea, laughing. "'So, listen' I told her, 'the cost is your firstborn child,' and she got all in a tizzy. Was I being so unreasonable?"

Though I am not experienced in these matters, I secretly

thought he was overcharging her. I stared him down over my tea, but I didn't answer his question. He has beautiful yellow eyes that make me forget what I am going to say.

"What's that look about? Well, what should I expect from a girl who charges two bits for a wish! Listen, I'm in the right! People always want something for nothing. It brings the whole profession down if you undervalue your work. So she whines about the price for a while, sobbing and carrying on and all the like, as if I'm going to fall for that! Well, I wasn't born yesterday, and she finally gets that into her pretty little head! So she agrees. I say the magic words, and siss-boom-bah-ta-da! Straw! Is! Gold!" He puffed up like a rooster. Funny little man! "Of course, her eyes nearly popped out of her pretty little head, the head which, incidentally, she was able to keep, courtesy of yours truly."

"She must be truly indebted to you." I could not help feeling a little nauseated.

"We'll find out," he snickered.

I bet her "pretty little head" isn't all that pretty. At least, I hope not. He started to leave, and I had the strangest sinking sensation.

"You know, *I* can conjure up a baby," I said.

"Really?" His eyebrows raised.

"Yes, really." I sipped my tea and pretended to be interested in something out the window. "Delicious ones."

"I'll be over again tomorrow."

I felt greatly relieved.

✳

The rest of the day was slow.

Put in a window box full of flowers. Mama would just die again if she knew! I'm trying not to think about her too much. I don't wish I was home, exactly, but I do wish the faces of people wouldn't fade so quickly. It's only been a little over a week, but I have to try hard to remember what Mama looks like, what Miss Harbinger looks like, what

Auntie Malice looks like. I run their faces through my mind, one by one, like tarot cards. When I do remember, they are frowning at me. So I work in the garden. Sunflowers never frown. At anybody.

The sound of the trees talking to each other in their confiding whispers make me ever lonelier. I sing to keep up my spirits.

"How do you learn when there isn't a book,
When there isn't a sign to lead you?
How will your hunger for knowledge be fed
When there isn't a spoon to feed you?
Should you look for a map in the sky?
Are the answers in stars that float by?
Is it easier still to comply
With the mores around that besiege you?
How do you learn when there's no one to trust
In the difference between right and wrong?
There's another voice there, in the ether somewhere,
Who is singing an interesting song.
If I listen close
I might find folks
Who have needed me all along."

I am comforted to think I have a little Auntie Malice in me, even if it is just a little.

Silver Nickel Moon, full

I decided that I needed to hang up some sort of a sign to increase traffic. I leaned up a broad piece of wood against the well and started painting.

Spells by the Well
one gold coin
(nonrefundable)

I stood up and looked into the well. It looked so dank and homey, I lowered myself in the bucket, down to the bottom. There were all sorts of lovely spiderwebs and mud puddles and even a bone or two, and I was so overcome with homesickness that I just crumpled into a corner and covered my head and cried and cried.

Mama came to me in full, not her angry face, but I could

smell her sweet sulfur perfume and hear her cackling laughter as she stomped on Clot's tail. I could see her by the hearth, stirring potions in the cauldron and muttering curses: *You'll be the wickedest witch wherever the four winds blow.* Just thinking about her made me gulp and gulp. I missed Mama, but I couldn't go back. How could I explain about sunflowers or cake or satisfaction to Mama? How do you explain those things to someone whose whole life is toil and trouble?

I don't know how long I was down there before I heard a voice call, "Yoo-hoo!"

"Who is it?"

"It's Goldilocks!" I hunched down further. "Who is talking to me?"

"It is I," I called, trying to disguise my voice, "the Witch of the Well. What are you doing way out here in the woods, Goldilocks?"

"I am losted," she replied.

"I am *lost*," I corrected her.

"Me, too," she said sadly.

"Oh, Goldilocks! Are you frightened? Are you hungry?"

"Nah," Goldilocks said. "I went into that chocolate-chip house and helped myself." Typical.

I enchanted the bucket from down in the well and sent it up. "Hop in, Goldilocks, and it will carry you home."

"Okay," she agreed. "Will it carry Glenda Glinka, too?"

"Yes." I couldn't help smiling. "You and Glenda Glinka. Now, when you get back, be sure to tell everyone there's a witching . . . I mean, a *wishing* well in the middle of the forest. Okay?"

"Okay! Thank you, Witch in the Well!"

After she left, I sat in the well until the bucket returned, thinking about a wishing well. It has a nice ring to it, don't you think?

Chapter nine of *Be the One with the Wand*: "Fake it till you make it."

Silver Nickel Moon, waning gibbous

It took three days before "Rumpie" came over again. I was angry with him for breaking his promise to see me sooner, but as he drew nearer, my anger drained away. He brought corn-flowers, isn't that sweet? He asked me if I was going to the

Devil's birthday, and I got all fluttery and was about to ask him if that was an invitation, but before I could, he said he wasn't—he's still busy helping that girl with the straw. I scolded him for even asking me such a question; of course it wasn't befitting of an F.G. to attend such a party. I couldn't help thinking, though, Auntie was right. It is nice to be invited.

I think Rumpie might have a problem with his ears because he didn't seem to hear me at all. "Very demanding king," he told me. "Room twice as large, full of straw. The girl was going absolutely loony with fretfulness. Boy, was she glad to see me!"

"She wasn't still upset about the firstborn thing?"

"Nah, she thinks she can get out of it by guessing my name. Like that's possible. NOT! Haw-haw-haw!" Ich, he brays just like a donkey!

"What do you mean, by guessing your name?"

"Ah, she was looking for a loophole, you know, a way out of our little agreement. So I told her if she guessed my name, she could keep her kid."

"Considering your name, I wouldn't say that that's much of an escape clause," I countered.

He just leaned back and stretched. "All's fair in love and war, and baby, this must be love! Woo-HOO!" I could feel the booger cookies I had eaten earlier start to spin in my stomach. "Speaking of babies, how about it?"

I narrowed my eyes at him. "What do you have?"

"One gold coin." He smiled.

"It brings the whole profession down if you undervalue your work," I reminded him.

This made him laugh out loud. He shook his finger at me, "Careful. Smart girls aren't pretty."

"That's not what I've heard," I said. I almost said, "I'm a witch, what do you expect?" and the shock of how ready I was to answer this way made me feel as confused as a bat in sunlight.

I told him I had a lot of work to do, and so he left. I conjured up two donkeys so I wouldn't miss his laughter so much. Cornflowers or not, I think I may have to pull the welcome mat out from under old Rumpie.

★

Wishcraft practice is going very well, thanks to my "wishing well" scheme. I have taken to wearing an old witch's hat; the wide brim catches coins very nicely down in the well. I learned painfully from experience: falling coins can really hurt. Some things you just don't learn in books, even in *Be the One with the Wand*.

On the first day I opened for business, the bucket started lowering down on the rope. "Hey! Cut that out!" I called up.

"Hunky, is that you?" Velvet's face cut into the circle of light at the top of the well. She was squinting hard to find me at the bottom. I was so pleased to see her.

"Yes, it's me!"

"Looks like you're doing *well,* ha-ha!"

"Ha-ha!" I answered.

"I knew it had to be you when Goldilocks said someone was granting wishes from a well! You are so clever! Listen, I know you're at work," she called down, "but I brought you some of your mother's brew! I told her I was buying it for my own lunch."

"Is she still mad?" I asked.

"What do you think? She's furious! She's like a walking volcano! Gosh, Hunky, your garden is looking great! Is that really your very own house?"

I was embarrassed that I hadn't invited her over. "Would you and the coven like to come over sometime? I wasn't sure if you were allowed. . . ."

"Allowed? Hello, Hunky! We are witches! We will sneak!"

Silver Nickel Moon, waning crescent

The past few days have been busy, if rudimentary. Traffic is steady. Sometimes I talk to the customers, sometimes I don't. I think it is very helpful that nobody can see me, because wishes are rather private and it seems more anonymous this way. Some of the wishes are so embarrassing, I wouldn't want anyone to know what I was wishing, either. Wolf came by. He wished for a grandmother costume. Sometimes I wonder about Wolf.

A lot of wishes have to do with changing someone's appearance. For example, Red Riding Hood threw a coin and called down, "My mother? She made me this red cloak? And I don't want to hurt her feelings, but, like, does she really expect me to wear this? So could I please have a jean jacket I can change into once I get to school?" That was easy enough. So was the villager who wanted to know how to dance on the day of his wedding. And the wife who wanted to stop yelling at her husband. I like granting these small, earnest wishes.

A lot of the village peasants ask for money, which is funny.

If they care so much about money, why are they throwing it down a well? I grant their wishes for beautiful homes, golden touches, and pots that never empty, but I have made a policy that wishes that I consider greedy or otherwise over the top will expire at midnight. I don't mind giving people a change of pace, but my goodness, someone's got to save them from themselves. Honestly, people don't think things through. They'll make short work for witches.

Then there was the smart boy who threw down a coin and wished for three more wishes. I told him to go ahead and make them. He did, and then I said, "There. You made three more wishes, just what you wished for!" He thought that was a good joke, and for being a good sport I took him into the house and gave him a piece of cake and a slingshot, and he was very happy.

Rumpie threw down a coin. "I want a baby!"

I threw the coin back up out of the well and yelled, "No sale!"

I heard him laughing as he walked away.

I come out of my well in the evening, when the light is soft and all the heads of my flowers are turned to the setting sun. I am coming to love my bed and my stove and my own little house. Slowly.

Cabbage Moon, waxing crescent

Today a heavy coin came down the well and hit me on the leg. Tooth fairy currency. "Yoo-hoo!" called a familiar voice.

"Goldilocks? Is that you?"

"Yes! It is I, O Witch of the Well. I have a wish."

"What is it?"

"Bring my big sister Hunky Dory back to me."

"I was . . . she was not your big sister!"

"Yes, she was! She was forced to play with me and was very impatient and made dresses for my dolls. That's a big sister."

"Well, I can't grant that wish," I grumbled.

"Why not?"

"I just can't, all right?"

"Then give me my money back!" She started to sound weepy. "I had to knock out my own tooth to get the money for that wish!"

"Isn't there anything else you want?" I pleaded. I really did want to grant a wish for her.

"Well," she said, fully recovered, "I have always wanted to be a witch."

"What? You have not!"

"Yes, I have. But not a bad witch. I want to be a good witch."

"There's no such thing as a good witch."

"Yes, there is. Hunky Dory was a good witch. And my Glenda Glinka is a good witch."

"Your Glenda Glinka is a doll," I reminded her.

"No. I take her everywhere and I boss her around and she always gets dirty. That's a little sister. I want us to be Glinda and Glenda, witch sisters. Change my name to Glinda so I match."

"That's two wishes," I pointed out, but gave in. "All right, Goldilocks, you will be Glinda, the Good Witch of the North. But not until you grow up."

"I can wait," she called down. "Thank you, wishing well."

I sat in the well, thinking, for a long time.

Cabbage Moon, first quarter

You'll never guess what! When I woke up this morning, there was a note stuck in between my toes! I am attaching it here, as it may be one of the most important letters I have ever received in the history of my being a fairy godmother.

Dear Fairy-Godmother-in-Training:

There has been a recent assessment of your current efforts to enter into the Fairy Godmothers' Guild, Storybook Chapter. Although we are most impressed with the ability you have demonstrated thus far, please be advised that membership in the guild is restricted to individuals who grant wishes and/or assist those of noble blood, i.e. kings, queens, princes, princesses, etc. If you meet this requirement, please submit appropriate paperwork for consideration (see attached) and possible certification. Thank you!

Sincerely,

Tooth Fairy

Regional Manager

The form consists of two essays: *Persons of Nobility Helped?* and *How Helped?* The exciting part is that they are "most impressed"! I really cooked up a humdinger when I brought the baby out of the well! I don't mean to brag, but I felt like a real fairy godmother then! It's a shame that it didn't qualify me for the Guild. I suppose I could submit that I helped baby Aurora, but I don't know if anyone really needs to know that I'm related to the infamous Spiteful Malice. Besides, that was more of an act of damage control than anything else. If you ask me, the whole thing is rather on the snobbish side. Who really cares, I suppose, if I'm official or not? I grant more wishes in a day than I bet most F.G.s do in a week! On the other hand, it wouldn't hurt. But where the heck will I find a princess around here? There's not a glass tower for miles.

There is only one person I can think of who gets around enough to know where I might find a princess, and like it or not, that's Auntie. I will look for her at the Devil's party. Should I leave a note for Rumpie to tell him I'm going? I guess not. He has Little Miss Straw-Head, doesn't he!

Old Devil Moon

It was a long walk to the Devil's party, but no problem to locate the festivities. I simply walked toward whatever the squirrels and chipmunks and deer and toads were running from. The party glowed and rollicked like a red beating heart deep within the body of the woods. It was even easier to find Auntie in the crowd. She was whirling like a dervish in her purple gown, her fetching owl-pellet earrings swinging, frothing up the crowd with an original score to the evening.

"No candle lit upon the cake,
But flames are in no short supply.
This must be it! The hour is nigh
For the Devil's birthday!

The guests are all horrific creatures:
Principals and piano teachers,
Drunken boors from baseball bleachers
At the Devil's birthday!

The moon, it cowers behind a cloud
To hide from such a gruesome crowd.
They're singing poorly, singing loud,
Hooray, the Devil's birthday!

The food has only partly died,
The dressing is formaldehyde,
The chef is all aglow with pride,
Yum yum, the Devil's birthday!

The gifts are melted chocolate, coals,
Shoes for cloven hooves, and moles,
Classrooms beyond all controls,
Three cheers, the Devil's birthday!

Hot Potato, Pin-the-Tail!
Popped balloons (they were on sale),
Black streamers hang to decorate.
Oh, don't you wish it were your fate
To attend the toast of the undertown?
Be bad! Perhaps next time around
You'll attend the Devil's birthday!
Yah-hah, the Devil's birthday!!
Hoo-hee, THE DEVIL'S BIRTHDAY!!"

There was a big buffet line with a steam table full of Southern-fried batwing, steamed poison ivy, and callus-and-corn-bread. It all made my mouth water, and my heart broke to smell the home-style cooking, but I didn't dare step forward. I hadn't been nearly bad enough to be invited and could not imagine what the motley would do if they spotted a turncoat in their midst, but even more so, what would Auntie say? I watched from behind a tree.

Music blared loudly, and Beelzebub was busy scratching some records on a turntable using his long fingernails. It has become a bit of a tradition to torture school board members who censor books by forcing them to listen to rap music. I must admit that I was glad I didn't miss it.

Beelzebub's voice sounded just dreadful, like a full toilet flushing, and of course the humans cowered, too thick to notice that the more they showed fear, the more he enjoyed himself. I know better than to be afraid of him: he's just a figurehead, half real goat and half scapegoat for all the evil people do to themselves with their stubborn lack of tolerance. I could hardly feel sorry for the victims, bothering poor uncle Beelzebub all year long, invoking his name over every little thing. Anyway, he usually sends them home after they've done a book report or two and promise not to bother him unless

it's over something that would interest him, like a video game.

*

A girl walked by wearing a very funky vintage outfit, black-and-white-striped stockings and a crooked pointy black hat. I liked her style, so I leaned forward. She noticed, stopped, and peered in my direction. I fell back into the shadows but the girl looked right at me and gasped, "Hunky Dory?"

I recognized the wonky teeth right away and motioned desperately for her to come over. "Is that you?" She was

wide-eyed. "I never would have expected to see you here!"

"Might say the same for you, Lemon." She looked from side to side and gently moved me farther behind a tree. "Look, I'm having some trouble. Maybe you can help me. Is there some book or something that can tell me how to be an F.G.?"

"You know what's funny? We use the very same book you use! *Be the One with the Wand.*" I was shocked. "Anyway, what would you need a book for? It's actually similar to being a witch in many respects." Lemon chewed thoughtfully at the end of her yellow braid. "Granting wishes is about giving people what they want, and casting spells is about giving people what they don't expect, but getting what you want never turns out like you expect, right? Half the time people want to undo what they wanted in the first place, or ask for dumb things that they obviously are going to need to undo later. It gets old fast, Hunky. It's all treat and no trick. Being a witch is so much more fun!" she cheered. "I can't believe you left the coven. Blech! Being an F.G. was so . . . *Girl Scout.*"

"Well, I do like cookies," I gulped, feeling the tips of my ears turning red.

"Mmmm," she said casually. "Well, anyway, thanks for bringing me to your school. You know what? After I bit that girl, I got the funniest feeling. All fizzy and good, but not *good* good, *bad* good. Really bad good!" Her pointy fairy eyebrows shot up fiendishly. "I guess I always had a little witch in me." She sipped her Choke-a-Cola and surveyed the crowd, dancing a little bit so her hat waggled. "Look at that girl over there! She's such a dork!" She cackled. It was Red Riding Hood, back in her cloak, being cornered by Pete Huckster, the devil who visited our class to tell us about barbecue sauce. "Just the other day, I caught her in the woods, changing out of her hoodie into a jacket, trying to be cool. Ha-ha! I turned the jacket into a blue monkey and let her wear that on her back for a while!"

I felt just terrible. If Lemon ruined her jacket, why didn't Red just come back and ask for another one? I guess she didn't want to seem greedy.

"Look at that basket! Who dresses her, her grand-mother?" said Lemon.

"Her mom made that cloak for her," I explained, and reminded her: "Chapter four, *Be the One with the Wand*: 'Don't be meaner than you have to be.'"

"My bad!"

"You *are* a witch," I said. Lemon kept her eyes steady on the crowd. "You are going to be very popular."

"'Popularity: The Devil's Virtue,'" Lemon recited. "I've been learning my lessons well, Hunky. Miss Harbinger is a good teacher." The thought of Lemon sitting on my toadstool back home, maybe passing notes to Velvet, gave me a funny pain in my chest, an aching. Lemon looked at me suddenly and apologetically, as if she could feel the ache. Her whole face changed, softened, and looked young again—less know-ing but more wise—as if she remembered for a moment what it was like to have feelings. Her teeth seemed less for biting, more silly and friendly, and I saw again the thing I had liked in her. Then she pulled it all back in, like a hermit crab crushing itself back into a shell that's too tight. She covered her teeth with her tongue, and her eyes left my face to scour the crowd of nameless black and red spirits. "So, I'm going to be popular? Is that your gift to me, Miss F.G.?"

"No," I said. "I think that's your curse."

"And what is *your* curse?" I turned around and there was Auntie Malice. I couldn't help it; I threw myself into her arms and hugged her, and she hugged me back and then hit me with her broomstick. "What are you doing here?"

"Oh, Auntie! I came to ask you where I might find a princess."

"Oh, no you don't! First fairy godmothers, now princesses? I'm not introducing you to any more riffraff! You're just too impressionable, you silly stupid girl! You stinking little goody-two-shoes! I hope you are coming home for good!"

"I can't," I whispered. The tears of joy I was shoving into the back of my eyes were dripping down my throat.

"Yes, you can." She spun around and admired the way her skirt flowed. "Your mother will get over it in a hundred years or so."

"And you? Have you gotten over it?"

"There's nothing for me to get over. I was expecting it. It was my gift to you when you were born."

"*What* was your gift?" My mind raced. "The ability to grant wishes?"

Auntie clucked her tongue. "No, you silly. *Conflict.* I gave you conflict! Problems. Confusion. *Drama!*"

"Wow!" said Lemon Droppings. "That is completely awesome! Why didn't I think of that! Child-care services, *pshaw!*" Auntie Malice minded her cuticle while she received the compliment.

"No, it is *not* completely awesome!" I stomped my foot. "Why would you do that?"

"To build *character!*" She waved her arm with a flourish and spun around again. "You will have my gift until it fully develops. What could be better than *character?* Why, people line up to see it, darling! Of course, it didn't turn out exactly the way any of us expected, but there's the *fun* of it. There's the *spice.*"

"The fun of it!" I don't think I have ever felt more exasperated in all my life.

"I don't see why you're so upset," Auntie Malice said. "Things have been going so well with you. Your wishing well is all the rage. Did you know that you've got copycats all over the county? Imitation is the sincerest form of flattery, darling! I am always flattered when people imitate me!"

111

"Anyway, 'there's more to you than the job you do,'" said Lemon Droppings. "*Be the One with the Wand,* chapter seven.'"

Auntie Malice patted Lemon on the tip of her pointy hat. "Who is this devastating creature?" she cooed. "I just love when people quote from my book."

"What do you mean, *your* book?"

"By my book, I mean *my book, Be the One with the Wand.* I wrote it so many years ago—oh, badness, I dare not tell you how many, ha-ha! Under the pen name, Venefica Mandrake. Hunky, you knew that, didn't you?" I could not even speak. "Oh, my goodness, didn't your mother ever tell you?"

"You are the author of that book? Miss Malice! I *live* by that book!" Lemon squawked like a parrot.

"Well, keep it under your pointy hat, dear," whispered Auntie. "I try to remain incognito. Nobody likes a show-off. Venefica Mandrake. Venefica Mandrake. Doesn't it have a nice ring to it? I think so."

"Does it bother you that F.G.s are using it?" I accused.

"Gracious, no! I don't care who buys it, just so long as they do. My fabulous lifestyle doesn't pay for itself, darling."

"Speaking of F.G.s, there's smoke coming out of your fingertips," Lemon pointed out in a whisper. "Not very good form for a fairy. Just FYI."

I ignored her and faced my aunt, speaking slowly and nearly shouting to make sure she heard every bit of the next question. "Well, if you thought character was so important, then why in Hades wouldn't you just give me the gift of character instead of the gift of conflict?"

Auntie stopped spinning, dumbfounded, and stared at me for a moment before she answered. "Because I am a *witch*, dear. *Obviously.*"

 Cabbage Moon, waning gibbous

Well, how's this for gratitude! You'll never believe what that Wolf did! He ate my house! What does he take me for, some little pig? He just sat there, looking sheepish, with his big fat tummy sticking out nearly a foot away from the rest of his body, with a big chocolate ring around his muzzle! I asked him why he did it. Woodcutter wouldn't let him eat Red Riding Hood, he complained, and he was sooo hungry.

Is that my problem? Well, now it appears to be. Needless to say, I have confiscated the grandmother costume. I am so furious, I am thinking of returning to the witches! What I really would like to do is lie down and cry, but that hoggy wolf ate my bed, too! It's a lucky thing I carry my wand and diary around with me, or I'd really be at a loss. He keeps pacing back and forth, saying, "I'm sorry! I'm sorry!" and burping! It's disgusting! Sometimes sorry just isn't enough. Twice without a home . . . it's all too much.

My head aches from crying. I must look a sight! I'll sleep in the well tonight.

Cabbage Moon, still waning gibbous

After much consideration in the well, I have arrived at some conclusions:

1. I am going to get exactly nowhere if I sit around and wait for fame and fortune to bite me on the toadstool, or look for support from others. I've got to seek success myself! That is why . . .

114

2. I will not build another house. I am off to become a real fairy godmother—not some two-bit corncob of a wish-granter. I'm talking about number-one fairy godmother, or bust! If there are no rules, I'll make them up as I go along.

Cabbage Moon, half empty

I'd been walking for miles, far out of the woods. The sun was very hot, and the day was sticky moist. I felt as though I was wading through a thick gravy. Still, the crickets chirped their encouragement all along the path, and the tall grass took even the smallest breeze and used it to make the sound of a great rain. I closed my eyes and let the music cool me, cheer me, and then I saw little houses not too much farther up along the hillside.

Suddenly, I was hit by a crab apple. Frantic Search jumped down from a tree.

"First time I've ever seen an apple jump away from a worm," I remarked.

"Have a good time at the birthday?" she jeered. "Lemon

said you showed up. I would have thought you were too good for such lowbrow theater."

"Leave me alone, Frantic."

"Are you sure you don't want to be on my mailing list? It'll keep you in the loop. I send some very in-ter-esting chain letters," she cackled.

Frantic's looks of disdain and contempt did nothing but set my powers percolating. She stuck her nose up in the air and started to pass me, swinging her derriere in an exaggerated way. I conjured up an egg, meaning to hit her with it, but I hesitated. She looked back at me as I crushed it in my own hand, black flesh and yolk running down my arm, my eyes never leaving hers. She ran from me too soon to see the egg in my other hand, which I gently cracked to produce a peeping chick.

Which hand will I use in this world?

Later

It's the middle of the night. Can't sleep. Thinking about Straw-Head. If she doesn't guess Rumpie's name, he'll take her baby. He means what he says. I wonder if he meant it when he said she had a "pretty little head." Did he say exactly that she was pretty? I can't quite remember. I bet he did. That stinker!

Perhaps I'll just go home and open a magic bakery. That wouldn't be bad. Breads and cakes, sugar-covered cookies, maybe a new cat to keep me company, too.

It just seems like I would be settling for less after all I have been through. But maybe that's just because I'm looking at myself through someone else's eyes. My ambition seems to fade with every step away from all that I built. "Don't work for other people when you can work for yourself." Chapter twelve, *Be the One with the Wand.*

I can't help it. It's a good book.

 # Cabbage Moon, waning crescent

That would really be a shame if she lost her baby, wouldn't it? It's really a cause for concern. People like her, they can't just draw up a baby from a well, after all. That Rumpelstiltskin is so inconsiderate! I've got half a mind to march right home and tell that stupid girl what her boyfriend's name is! And I bet he is her boyfriend!

Later

I'm going home. I'm going to tell that girl Rumpelstiltskin's name. I'm pretty annoyed about the whole thing, and to tell you the truth, quite inconvenienced. Signs are being posted around a nearby village. Some prince is going to have a ball. A prince—if I could help him, I could be certified! And I bet there aren't many other F.G.s around these parts, either. It has been a real dilemma. Shall I pursue my career to the fullest, or go running back to help some stupid girl who doesn't have sense enough not to make deals with trolls? My head says let her wallow in the muck! But my conscience won't allow it. There's a baby at stake, after all, and I do rather like babies. Maybe I'll just stroll through the village on my way back, see if that prince is around. I'm entitled, aren't I?

Later, and
I'm still up

No prince to be found—just a lot of proclamations about the ball. I'm pretty much the only woman walking around, the rest are getting all gussied up. Through the windows I can see them preening, twirling in their skirts like drunken ballerinas. It seems that the prince is going to choose a bride at the ball. Imagine that, being herded together like a bunch of cattle in evening gowns so the big bull can pick his favorite heifer! Enough to make anyone sick. I'll be glad to miss him, after all. If helping the likes of him is what the Guild considers the makings of a noble profession, well, we just don't see eye to eye. Still, I wouldn't mind a party, nice dresses, food and all. I wonder what it's like to be pretty, princess material. But it's no use wondering, because I'll never know. I wish I didn't have such a large wart on my nose. Maybe it's not so big to other people, but it is to me. Sigh! Well, I'll never be a truly great fairy godmother if I'm so self-involved—although I am beginning to wonder if I stand a chance of being a truly great fairy godmother at all. Rumpie is in a better position to get certified than I am!

After all, he's helping Straw-Head, and if she becomes queen, then . . .

Wait a second. That's right! If I tell her Rumpie's name, and she becomes queen, wouldn't that be the same as granting a wish for royalty? And I can save the baby to boot!

I've got to get home!

 # Honey Moon, new

Wow, what a night I've had! You won't believe it!

I headed out of town at dusk. Nobody was around—there was a carriage here and there, but they drove off quickly. Everyone was in a hurry to get to the ball. The only other creature out and about was a little black cat who reminded me of Clot. Melancholy weighed so heavily in my heart, I thought I would cry. I thought I *was* crying, but actually it was some girl sitting at her fireplace. Her doleful wails carried right up the chimney! Good thing everybody was gone, or she would have roused the whole neighborhood. I wasn't in the most pleasant mood, so I first thought, "I'm in a hurry! No time for nonsense!" but then the girl really let out a howl, and I found myself knocking at her door. She was too busy hyperventilating to answer, so I let myself in. When she saw me, her eyes grew very wide.

"You must be my fairy godmother!"

Talk about Presumptuous with a capital P! "That has not yet been determined," I answered coolly. "I'm rather in a hurry."

"Oh, please help me!" She grabbed on to the edge of my skirt, and proceeded to delve into a most dreadful life story. It seems that her mother is dead, and her jellyfish of a father has married a tyrant of a woman with two hideous and ill-natured daughters who treat the poor girl like a veritable slave. On top of everything, they call her Cinderella—after the cinders in the fireplace that are her duty to sweep out. So why doesn't she call those sisters a name or two? It seems she wasn't all that assertive, except when it came to *me*.

"Please, please help me!" she whined. "Everybody's at the ball but me. They wouldn't let me go."

"What do you want me to do, turn your stepsisters into mudskippers?" I waved my wand around a bit, just warming up, but Cindy grabbed my wrist.

"No, no! I just want to go to the ball and have a wonderful memory to sustain me for the rest of my miserable lifetime."

I told her what I thought of the prince's ball, giving her my bull-heifer theory, but she was unmoved and unconvinced. "You're your own worst enemy," I warned her. "If I give you a hand with this ball thing, I hope you don't let that awful prince get too fresh."

"I'm sure that the prince won't be looking at meee." She giggled foolishly.

I had half a mind to leave her in her soup, but no sooner had she giggled than the laughter had turned into weeping and wailing again, so I told her to hush up, for goodness' sake, and get me a pumpkin.

I turned the pumpkin into a carriage and some field mice into a team of horses, and like that. Rudimentary stuff. Then I gave her a dress as pink and fluffy as cotton candy, a tiara fit for a real princess, long white gloves with buttons up the sides, silk stockings . . . the works! She would turn every head at that cheap dance hall of a castle, I'll tell you that!

"My shoes! I haven't any shoes," she squealed. How's that for appreciation?

"I suppose you'll need them, with the prince stomping on your toes all evening." So I gave her some slippers made of crystal, except for the toes, which were Plexiglas.

She whirled around and around, looking as lovely as a birthday cake. She kissed me on the cheek and held both my hands, her eyes aflame with gratefulness or hysteria, I couldn't tell which. No rocket scientist, that one. I reminded her to be home at a reasonable hour, to which she barely nodded yes. It will be a miracle if she takes the most valuable gift I offered—my advice!

Later

I'm really kicking myself for helping that Cinderella girl out! Now I'm totally behind schedule! My skateboard flies fast, but not as fast as Rumpie works! Straw-Head doesn't stand a chance.

 ## Honey Moon, waxing crescent

Went to see Straw-Head. She was beautiful, just as I suspected. I told her Rumpelstiltskin's name, but she said she already knew; some messenger overheard him singing about himself. Typical! She was very nice about it, saying that she appreciated my coming to tell her anyway. I can see why Rumpie likes her. That stinker!

So there it stands. I came all the way back to the woods from a village rife with possibilities for career advancement just so I could rat on my friend. Was I wrong to try to be a fairy godmother? Was it wrong to try to help Straw-Head? It's so hard to know.

I built a temporary lean-to out of pretzels because I was tired. So tired, I fell asleep. I woke up in the same old woods. Everything has come full circle. It all seems so meaningless. I feel like my heart is a gift, but I have no one to give the gift to. Not Mama. Not Rumpie. Not anyone. Now what? "If you're between a rock and a hard place, stand still." Chapter five, *Be the One with the Wand.* I think. Too weary to check.

 Honey Moon,
waning gibbous

Standing still has its benefits. You know, you can learn a few things by watching TV. I was zoning out over a *This Old Haunted House* marathon to drown my sorrows, and I got a little inspired, in spite of myself. I made a mosaic cornice out of bone and broken plates and bits of silver mirror. I even started on the kitchen, filling baskets with herbs and hanging them from the pretzel loops in the ceiling. Then I smashed a hole in the side of the wall for a window. That felt good.

Honey Moon,
waning crescent

I planted some lollipops in the yard (we'll see what happens) and hung colored bottles on the juniper tree. They do this in the Bahamas, you know, to capture evil spirits. I could use the company.

My coven-ection oven finally arrived in the mail. I was able to pay for it using the money I've been saving from the well, and I got a good deal online because the last gingerbread boy that was baked in it ran off. And guess what else came in the mail? A letter from Cinderella! What a surprise!

Dearest Fairy Godmother,

Thanks for the help. The ball was fun, but you were right about the prince. All hands and sugar talk! Between that and those uncomfortable shoes you whammied up, by midnight I was plenty ready to leave! That prince was after me like a tiger after a T-bone, but I outran him! Lost one of the shoes, which he kept! Now he's looking for me. What a weirdo! I'm going to lay low for a while until this thing blows over.

Stepsisters still as mean as ever. I saw them at the ball, but they didn't recognize me. I look different when I smile, and they never see me smile. Do you look different when you smile?

Love,

Cinderella

p.s. Hey, want to be pen pals?

I'll have to think about being pen pals. I checked my reflection in the nearby pond. It looks about the same whether I am smiling or not. I guess I have a pleasant face.

 # Honey Moon, still waning crescent

The pastry on the apple fritters came out so flaky when I brushed it with egg white. I cut out little bat cookies. Why not? What if a little witch girl should happen by? I wished that Goldilocks would have appeared at the doorway with Glenda Glinka to help me shake the chocolate sprinkles. I wished it so hard that I looked up at the doorway. But nobody was there.

While I turned the batter in my bowl, I thought of my

mother, stirring, stirring in her kitchen. It occurred to me that it is a horrible day when you discover that the people you always thought were very happy are really not so happy after all. Then it is another horrible day when you realize you're not all that different from the people you think are unhappy.

I guess when that happens, all that's left to do is to invent what happiness means all over again, from scratch. That's why I'm baking; it's the only thing I really know how to do from scratch. I'm tired, but starting over is still easier than going down the wrong path. Just ask Red Riding Hood.

That's not from *Be the One with the Wand*.

That's from me.

 # Honey Moon, over

Rumpie found me in my new house. He went wild when he saw me. "Where have you been? Where did you go? I missed you so much!" On and on. It was very flattering, but I maintained my composure. I asked him how it went with Straw-Head, and he said, "Not so good." I immediately felt guilty, even though I didn't exactly do anything, and I started preparing him a big pot of mashed potatoes with extra butter.

"I liked her at the start, but after a while, I felt so . . . unappreciated," he complained. Join the club, I thought. "I turned out more vaults of gold than a fleet of ships could carry, but she started getting so casual about it. She started bringing her girlfriends over while I was changing straw into gold. They would knit, and do each other's hair, and play Monopoly . . . Do you think they would ask me to play?" He grunted bitterly. "They would gossip, gossip, gossip. Little Bo-Peep *this!* Little Boy Blue *that!* Then, nag, nag, nag! 'Your beard's getting too long, can't you trim it here or there?' 'Your gold isn't as shiny, can't you buff it up a bit?' 'Can't you be more polite in front of my friends?' 'Oh, goodness, get along now, here comes the king!'" Rumpie took such a high-pitched, wheezy tone when he mimicked her, I smiled in spite of myself. He smiled, too, but it was a crooked smile.

I dished him up a big bowl of potatoes before I spoke. "Listen, Rumpie, I . . . I told her your name."

He looked at me, shrugged, then looked in his lap. "Doesn't matter. Her first guess was 'George,' and I told her she was right, and went on my merry way. Her baby probably would have been colicky anyhow."

We were quiet for a moment, digesting mashed potatoes and sour grapes.

"I'm sorry, I know you liked her."

"Not as much as I like you." He smiled. My heart jumped suddenly, surprising me. "Looks aren't everything, after all."

Is that his idea of a compliment? I felt my brain talk to my heart. Luckily, my brain is a great motivational speaker. My heart calmed down.

He leaned over the table and narrowed his eyes and smiled in a distinctly snaky way.

"Call it amnesia,
But when I see'd ya
My heart did things I didn't know that it could do!
You've gone from wallflower to stunning ingénue!
I've forgotten what I didn't like about you."

I cleared my throat, and wished for the first time that Auntie's gifts were genetic.

"Oh, Rumpie, you'd be first in line to get some play,
If only I had been born just yes-ter-day.

130

It turns out I've got not only your name, but your number,
So may I wish good luck to you
in finding someone slightly dumber?
A princess you may have traded,
But since we last met, my standards have upgraded.
The things I like are things I should have hated.
I remember what it was I didn't like about you."

"It's become increasingly relephant,
You've got memory like an elephant,
But to pachyderms I have to say, pooh-pooh!
Call it forgetfulness,
But I'm positive you're the best,
The fairy who could make my wish come true,
Your wiles could make sticky tape unglue!
It seems I can't recall that there was anything at all
I didn't like about you."

"I wish amnesia were contagious,
'Cause your behavior was outrageous
And I still recall the way you made me blue.
The prospect of me in your arms
Is setting off some loud alarms.

I think that I would rather have the flu.
I remember very clearly what it was I didn't like about you."

"Like what?"
"You're inconsiderate."
"What else?"
"You are a boor."
"That's all?"
"You've been the layover on my world tour.
The fly in my soup, oh, waiter!
I should bid you see you later,
But I seem to be remembering
That something else is true:

Call it amnesia
But when I see'd ya
You made me laugh and smile like no one else could do.
I can't dismiss that you're a devil,
But we could be friends forevil—oops, I mean forever.
If I remember,
And I'll try hard to remember,
It may take some time to remember
what it is that I like about you."

The fire was extinguished from Rumpie's eyes, but not the friendship.

I poured him another cup of tea, and then hit him in the head with the gourd full of toe jam. Not because I'm a witch. But because I felt like it.

 Cream Pie Moon, waxing crescent

Good Wishes to Grant (list for reference)

Babies
Friends
Health
Peace
Clarity
Confidence
Second chances
Aspirin
Free time
Talent
Baked goods
Character (I guess)

Cream Pie Moon, waxing gibbous

I figured how to make the icing for petit fours. They were a hit! Seven dwarfs came by and cleaned me out. They didn't seem the least bit interested in the samples of apple fritters. I can't imagine why not. Oh, well, can't win 'em all. Tomorrow: on to banana éclairs!

Cream Pie Moon, full

Guess who came by? My coven showed up, with Velvet holding a pot of marigolds in a decidedly uncomfortable way. "You look totally the same!" she announced.

"I haven't been gone that long," I reminded her.

"It seems like decades," she groaned.

"Your place is totally cute!" Frantic looked around. "Ew!"

"I like the spiderwebs in the corner," Velvet smiled, giving Frantic a *behave yourself* look. "Nice touch." I didn't have the heart to tell her I didn't put them there on purpose. "Whee!" Velvet hooted down the front hall, spinning to see if it echoed. "It's so grown-up, Hunky! It's so big and airy!"

"If you like air," Frantic said. "I think building your own house is kind of boyish. Aren't you afraid people will think of you as, like, some kind of warlock or something?"

"Miss Harbinger said girls could do it," Velvet reminded her. "Or weren't you paying attention?"

If she had been paying attention then, she wasn't paying attention now. Her eyes slid suspiciously from the curtains to the bouquet on the table to the mosaic doorway I had been putting together out of broken teacups. "Well, if anyone's looking for a sunflower or a bluebird, I'll know where to send them," she grumbled.

"I hear you've started a bakery," Lemon said.

"Do you think it's a good idea?" asked Frantic. "I mean, you've got to be careful. Your *figure* and all. You already look a bit like a stuffed bun."

"Yeah, it's a good idea," I told her. "I have regular customers and still have time to grant wishes. It's a crossover market. Hungry people are wishful people."

"Very enterprising," said Sinus.

135

"Hunky's mom is very enterprising, too." Velvet turned to Lemon. "You know, she has the greatest collection of dolls. They're, like, her hobby. Do you have any of those cool dolls, Hunky?"

"No, I keep the place a little less . . . cluttered," I said, thinking how nice Befana would look on the shelf by the window. Suddenly I realized how long it had been since I'd gone to a cellar sale.

"When I get my own place, I want one just like yours. Only I'm going to have stalactites and stalagmites everywhere. And an underground river." Velvet plopped down into an armchair. "And newts. Lots of newts."

"Where's your cat?" Belladonna bent to look under a chair.

"I don't have a cat," I told her.

"You mean you live here all by yourself?" She gasped. "Aren't you lonely?"

"Sometimes," I confessed. The witches looked at me with a mix of admiration and pity. "But Rumpelstiltskin comes around pretty regularly."

"Rumpelstiltskin? You mean that gorgeous troll who spoke to our class is your boyfriend?" Belladonna gasped.

"No, no, no," I corrected her. "He's my friend. He's my friend who's a boy."

"Oh, come on," begged Twisted Ankle. "We're all grown-up. You can tell us."

"If you're really grown-up, you know that witches and trolls can be just friends," I repeated. "He's been giving me a hand around the house, and sometimes I cook for him."

"If you're just friends, then you won't mind giving him my number." Frantic smiled her snakey smile.

"Sure, it's your funeral." I went into the kitchen for refreshments, glad that Frantic wouldn't have the satisfaction of seeing me grimace. I didn't feel jealous, exactly, but still, I felt my lips silently sounding out about ten different comebacks: Your number is not one I would give a friend. I think we all have your number, Frantic. You're a number-one . . .

I laid out the tea. My friends looked at each other, unsure of what to do. I threw the teacup at Lemon's head, hitting her. Velvet pitched her cup at me, but I ducked and it smashed against the wall. Then Lemon splashed the contents of her cup into Frantic's face. She sputtered and gasped. We all sighed and laughed. I poured new cups of tea for us to really drink.

"Aren't you going to get in trouble for coming here?" I asked.

"Terrible trouble!" chirped Velvet. "If anyone finds out."

"Which they will." Acid Reflux smiled. "Because I'll tell on you. I need the extra credit."

"I don't." Frantic slurped her tea.

"So how's the fairy godmothering going?" asked Lemon. "Bored yet?"

"Not at all," I said. "I'm still learning something new every day."

"Must be a real roller-coaster ride." Frantic suppressed a yawn, making her nostrils flutter. Then she perked up. "Want some practice?"

"What do you mean?"

"Grant me a wish!" said Frantic.

"*Frantic!*" Velvet put down her tea.

"Come on! I'll trade you a wish for a curse."

Lemon just barely shook her head no, trying to send a secret signal.

"I don't think so." I hoped Frantic would change the subject. She didn't. "Chicken," Frantic teased. "Bawk *bawwwwk*."

I sighed. "Real mature, Frantic."

"Anyway, she'd curse someone herself if she really wanted to, wouldn't you, Hunky?" Velvet attempted to come to my rescue.

"I guess so," I admitted. "If I got mad enough."

"Let's say what we would wish for, just for fun." Velvet hopped up and down. "I would wish for a lifetime supply of newts. What would you wish for, Lemon?"

"Gift certificates." Lemon rolled her eyes.

"If I were you, I'd wish to get my wonky teeth fixed," said Frantic.

A strange look came over Lemon; her cheeks got rosy, and I knew Frantic had guessed her real wish. I felt shades of my old self fall over me like a black curtain.

"If I were you, I'd wish to get my wonky brain fixed," I suggested.

"Some fairy godmother," snarked Frantic. "Loses her temper. That must be ugly."

"Yes, it is," I informed her coolly. It occurred to me that I didn't even know why Frantic was there. We weren't exactly friends in school.

"Ohh, is the fairy godmother losing her temper?" asked Frantic. "I'm so scaaaared."

"Why'd you come over, anyway?" I asked.

"I told you, I want a wish."

"So do I," I snapped. "I wish you'd go home."

Twisted tried to disguise a laugh as a cough.

"Too bad you can't grant your own wishes." Frantic smiled. "That's the deal, isn't it?"

"Not exactly," I said craftily. "I usually get what I want by giving people what they want." I looked over at Lemon, who was leaning forward, listening intently. She gave an almost imperceptible nod. *Frantic wants it that badly? Let her have it.* "So. Just for argument's sake. What would you like?"

"To be head of the class?" offered Acid.

"I'm already head of the class," sneered Frantic.

"No you're not," Velvet chirped back loyally. "Hunky's head of the class!"

"How can she be head of the class when she's not even in the class? Honestly, Velvet, you're not the sharpest wand in the box, are you?"

I felt the black curtain fall farther.

"If Hunky came back, you wouldn't be, Frantic. You'd be second best," Belladonna reminded her cheerfully. "And you are coming back, Hunky, aren't you? I'm sure Miss Harbinger would forgive you."

"She even said the other day that wand-wielders should stick together," said Sinus. "That there might be jobs in our generation that she couldn't have predicted that will require more wishery than witchery."

140

"Yes, wasn't that shocking?" laughed Twisted. "Who says you can't teach an old cat new tricks?"

"She must feel very bad about what happened." Velvet looked sincere. "Honestly, Hunky, it hasn't been the same without you."

Fear sparked in Frantic's eyes. What would happen if I said yes? Maybe her head would explode! That would be fun. I knew her wish very well. I thought of agreeing to come back, just to torture her. But speaking as someone who was formerly head of the class and fell from grace like a sack of bricks, I knew that being the best wasn't something that would last. As someone who lived without a coven, someone who competed with a girl I didn't even know for the attention of a boy I didn't even like, I knew that personal best is the only best there really is; that there's no use comparing yourself to anyone else. Miss Harbinger's words came back to me: "Developing a personal voice in one's work is all one really can aspire to." Poor Frantic really does want to be the best, I realized. She thinks there's such a thing. I felt so very sorry for the girl scowling in front of me. The black curtain lifted.

"I know what your wish is," I informed her.

"How could you know?" sneered Frantic. "I didn't even say it."

"It's familiar, that's how."

"So grant it, then," challenged Frantic.

"I don't think it's a good idea," I said. "You're wishing for something that isn't real. You're wishing for something that won't last."

"Just give it to me, Hunky!"

"Oh, give it a rest, Frantic!" Belladonna stomped her foot. "This isn't fun anymore! Let's do makeovers! I want green hair. Wouldn't I look awful with green hair!" She ran over to the big mirror I have hanging in my hallway and grabbed the ends of her matted mane, swaying coyly.

"Fine." Frantic got up and stood in front of the mirror. "Come on, Lemon. Don't you want to take a gander at those spectacular beaver teeth of yours?" Lemon got up and flicked Frantic on the back of her head with her thumb and forefinger. "Ow!" Frantic winced. We all peered into the mirror. "Brains *and* ugliness," said Frantic, preening. "I don't blame you for being jealous. It just isn't *fair*."

"It's the fairest," came a voice.

We looked around.

"What is?" asked Lemon.

"Not what is," said the voice. "Who is. Fairest of them all. Frantic Search." The mirror clouded and stirred itself in rippling waves. A ghostly floating head appeared. "Yowza," it said. "You put perfection in my reflection."

"Me?" Frantic pointed to herself. We all hid behind her.

"Yes, you. Fairest of them all. You're all that and a bag of chips."

"Oh, go on!" Frantic grinned, and the mirror grinned back. Frantic crossed her arms. "No, I mean it! Go on!"

The mirror looked surprised and cleared his throat. "Ummm . . . you're the fairest of them all."

"You said that," she sneered. "Am I uglier than her?" She

pointed accusingly to Belladonna, who stared at the mirror with wide eyes.

"Sure," said the mirror.

"That's *definitely* a matter of opinion," Lemon pointed out.

It did occur to me that maybe the mirror needed glasses. Belladonna's black hair is as tangled as a clogged sink and is the envy of every witch at school, and her blood-shot eyes are as red as scabs. She could stop traffic.

"Careful, Frantic," Belladonna sounded afraid. "'There's no voice on the outside that can tell you more than the voice on the inside.' *Be the One with the Wand*, chapter eight."

"Oh, you've always been a jealous little beast." Frantic waved her off. "Now, what about them?" Frantic motioned at us with her thumbs.

"No contest," said the mirror. "You're the ugliest and smartest and fairest of them all."

"You don't have to be so quick about it," Lemon snarled into the mirror. "One good rock and you've had it."

"Lemon Droppings, don't you dare! This is Hunky's present to me, isn't it, Hunky! Oh, I just love it, it's perfect! Thank you!"

"That mirror is going to get tired of lying," Velvet whispered.

"Once, I vowed to use her own rapacious cravings as a map to her own destruction," I confessed. "A promise is a promise."

"Oh, Hunky! You are the wickedest fairy godmother wherever the four winds blow," she breathed.

 # Cream Pie Moon, last quarter

Shocking letter from Cinderella!!

> *Dear Fairy Godmother,*
> *Hey, guess what! The prince found me! It turns out I'm the only one in the village with a size three foot. But don't worry, I straightened him out about some things. I consented to marry him and help rule the land. I have decided that success is the best revenge.*
> *Love,*
> *Your Cindy*

Hmmm, maybe she's not as goofy as I thought. I think I'll

write back, but not until I send a letter of congratulations to my friends, the woodcutter with the ax that never dulls and my friend with the baby that I pulled up from the magic well. They sent me a wedding announcement. I hope they will let me bake the wedding cake! Bakery business, by the way, is on the rise, ha-ha. Excuse me, can't elaborate now, the postman has returned. Wonder what it could be?

 Cream Pie Moon, still last quarter

Look at what came, special delivery! I am stapling it here to keep forevermore!

Dear Fairy Godmother (pending):
    Congratulations! Welcome to the Fairy Godmother Guild, Storybook Chapter. Upon coronation of Princess Cinderella, you will receive all honors due to you as an Official and

Certified Fairy Godmother, including
the grant of one wish for personal
purposes. Once again, welcome to the
profession of giving and granting.

Best Wishes,
Tooth Fairy
Regional Manager

My eyes are crossed, and I can hardly breathe.

Cream Pie Moon, waning crescent

I invited Lemon over. Who else could help me celebrate? Nobody else even knows what it means. We sat out on the veranda, lazily watching the fireflies hover and flash their green signals to one another. I reached into my apron and offered Lemon a piece of violet gum, which she accepted. Then she reached into her pocket and pulled out a box of beetles and offered one to me. "Thank you," I said.

"You're not welcome," she said.

"You're very good at this, you know," I told her, crunching my beetle. "It didn't take you any time at all to learn to be a witch."

"Miss Harbinger helps." She made a long purple rope with her gum. "And may I say, you can take the fairy godmother out of a witch, but you can't take the witch out of the fairy godmother."

"You must have been one heck of a fairy godmother," I had to say.

"Nah." She smiled. "I was lazy."

"But you were certified," I pointed out.

"Of course I was," she said. "I worked in a castle; there was royalty asking for about a zillion things a day so it was no big whip."

"So you got a free wish!" I realized.

"I didn't use it," she said.

I was shocked, but Lemon seemed hypnotized by the uneven blinking of the fireflies and spirals of gnats.

"Wasn't there anything you wanted?"

"Sure, there was." She turned to me. "But anything worth wishing for is worth going out and getting for yourself. Grant your own wishes, Hunky Dory." She snapped her gum. "I think I read that in a greeting card somewhere."

She picked at a burr stuck to her dress. We didn't speak for a long time.

"Just for fun, though. What would you wish for?"

"Straight teeth." She smiled her wonderful wonky smile. "Like Frantic said."

"You're crazy. Even I wouldn't grant that wish," I admitted.

"Then, a friend," she said. "A friend who would like me for who I am, wonky teeth and all. But I don't need to use up the wish for that, either."

"A lot of wishes are made because of impatience," I told her. "A lot of children wish they were grown up. That's a dumb one."

"No, it's not," said Lemon. "But it's not the real wish. I've noticed that wishes have a kind of a . . . a husk that has to be pulled away to reveal the deeper wish, the true and golden wish, the wish that the wisher didn't even know they wanted. Boy, F.G.s who grant those, they're the real McCoy."

"What do you mean, the husk of a wish?"

"Well, for instance, when children wish for growing up, they're not really after the age and the height. They are really wishing for respect and responsibility. They are wishing for the chance to grant their own wishes, too. So children are actually very smart. The chance to grant your own wishes is really the only wish worth making, Hunky."

"But growing up doesn't always mean all that," I pointed out.

"They don't know that," she reminded me. "Not knowing is not the same as being dumb." She shifted in her seat. "Let's try. Pretend you are just some regular workaday peasant, living in a cottage in the woods, with no special powers. What would you wish for? Just off the top of your head?"

I shut my eyes tight to think. Let's see. Was there anything I needed for the house? "Maybe a pet," I suggested. "Some sort of cat."

"See, *that's* dumb! You can get a stray anywhere. No sense using up a wish on that, and you know it. Even a peasant would be smart enough to wish for a cat that coughs up diamond hairballs or something." We smiled. "That wish is the husk. Pull it away. *Why* do you want a cat?"

"Because I'm lonely sometimes," I said slowly, unsure if Lemon would laugh at me. She didn't.

"Who are you lonely for? Who do you miss?"

I gulped. "My mother," I said. "Don't you?"

"Not really. I wasn't used to her being around. My mother was an actress," she said. "Queen Mab."

"No way!"

"Way." Lemon spit her gum out over her shoulder, then took out another beetle. "Busy woman. No time for me. She was on the circuit. Got me a gig at the castle as soon as she could, then off she flew. Or fluttered. Whatever." Lemon was getting that pulled-in look she sometimes gets.

"Wow," I said. "My mom is nothing like that. She hardly ever leaves the cave. She just works and works and works. Auntie is the glamorous one. Mama never travels or goes to parties. I can hardly remember her doing anything but standing over the cauldron."

"Your life must really freak her out, then." Lemon smiled.

I thought about this for a moment before asking Lemon, "Where's your mother now?"

"Who knows?" she said, her head turned away as though she were asking the air. *Who knows? Do you know, wind? Do you know, sky?* She didn't seem to expect an answer. She stared out over the meadow, as if she could see her mother emerge from the woods, like a beautiful ghost—appearing, and then fading—until her own daughter had to grasp at memory like bits of floating pollen; grasp just to remember the color of her own mother's eyes. "Where's yours?"

"Still in the cave, I expect. Cursing my name."

"Then you're lucky," said Lemon. "You know where to find her."

✳

I told Lemon she could stay with me for a while. Listening to her snoring, I thought about our conversation late into the night as I watched two field mice nibbling in the corner of my house. I tried to do what Lemon said: pull at the husk to find the true and golden wish. I do know where to find my mother, so why don't I go? Sure, I was mad that she'd thrown me out. But now, I am even more afraid she'll take me back in. Oh, she was so unpleasant. Always working, always yelling, always mad at somebody for doing something wrong. So many rules that could be broken, so many reasons not to forgive. So easily disappointed.

But then again, I know she was so proud of me. How excited she was to have a daughter at the head of the class. She always threw it in Frantic Search's mother's face. What did she imagine I would do once I graduated? *You'll be the wickedest witch wherever the four winds blow. . . .*

I thought about Mama, in that damp cave. Alone. While here I am, in this lovely place, with friends who visit me and

152

stories to tell, even though I'm barely a hundred years old! Maybe if Mama were happy, we'd have more in common. Maybe I should wish she were happy all the time. For some reason, though, that seemed creepy, even to me, who was formerly a witch. No, she didn't need to be happy. She just needed something to cheer her up.

She needs a wish, I thought. She needs a wish more than I do.

I wasn't sure how to go about it; the letter wasn't very specific. So I just lay in bed and said it. "I wish my mother could have her wish," I wished. "Her true and golden wish that lies under the husk. The wish that I don't know she wants. The wish *she* might not know she wants. The wish that I can give her without changing who I am. The wish that will bring us back together. And . . ." I added carefully, "the wish that nobody ever fully regrets having granted. If Mama has such a wish, under her crusty old husk, I wish it could be granted."

Well, I figured that the wish was too long and there was no way it would be processed, but then I got that feeling, that prickly feeling, that prickly feeling *all* over, even my teeth seemed to be electric, and I knew I had been granted a very, very big wish.

So I am writing because I can't sleep.
I wonder what I did.

Glowering Moon, new

I know I always say you'll never guess what happened, but today you'll *really* never guess what happened.

I went back to Mama's cave. I kept panicking, but I cast a spell on my legs to keep walking until I got there, so at least I couldn't turn back. Clot was sitting outside, and she yowled and hissed when she saw me and her back got all Halloweeny. It was good to be home.

Mama had hung up a big cage with a raven's skeleton inside at the opening of the cave, which I thought was very unfriendly, but not so bad as the doormat that said "WE DON'T WANT ANY." The knocker was a little brass face of an imp sticking his tongue out. I knocked.

Mama opened the door, took one look at me, and slammed it in my face before I could even say "Mama." I heard her shuffle away, but I just stood there, because, what was I supposed to do? I was so shocked. Then I heard her shuffle back, and the door opened, and there was my mother with a BABY in her arms. She held it straight out in front of her like it was garbage that needed taking out and then she demanded "What! Is the meaning! Of THIS!" She thrust the baby into my face.

I felt like I had a pinecone in my throat; I absolutely couldn't speak. I just stared at the baby, the funny little baby that was so squishy and sweet and smelled so deliciously nasty.

"ANYONE knows that the only way for a witch to get a baby is for someone to wish it on her! And I think we all know whose forté THAT is!"

My mind raced.

Her true and golden wish that lies under the husk.

The wish that I don't know she wants.

The wish she might not know she wants.

The wish that I can give her without changing who I am.

The wish that will bring us back together.

And, the wish that nobody ever fully regrets having granted.

"Goo," said the baby.

"Goo? Is he saying goo again?" Auntie Malice appeared in the doorway and took the offending object from my mother's hands. "*What* are you trying to *say*? I don't know

155

what 'goo' means. I have absolutely no idea what this person is trying to say! Now, Hunky, come in. Let's not hang our dirty laundry out here in the woods where all those gossipy owls can hear."

"No, Hunky may NOT come in!" My mother's face got as red as a blister.

"Now, now, there's plenty of time to decide whether or not she can come in after she's in." Auntie ushered me into the living room. "But, Hunky, you've really gone too far this time. This baby doesn't even speak the same language as we do. And the things that come out of that baby's behind are about a million times more foul than anything I could have concocted in my cauldron."

"Honestly, I had no idea . . ." I began. "I mean, I didn't wish Mama would have a baby." This was true. Sort of.

"This is not your mother's baby," Auntie corrected me. "This is *my* baby."

Auntie Malice's baby! My mouth dropped open with a clunk.

"Well, I really didn't wish Auntie would have a baby!"

"Well, somebody did!" Mama shrieked.

"Could have been anyone, really. What is the world coming to? Once again, I am the hapless victim of a nefarious society," Auntie Malice said absently, bouncing the child on her knee until he spit up. "Look! Look! He did it again!" she cheered. "Second time this morning! He's so talented! Honestly, something's always coming out one end or the other!"

Mama bent over and eyed the child skeptically, pulling the hair on her chin. "Wellll . . ." she said.

"You wouldn't begrudge me, sister, would you? After all, you have Hunky! And here am I, all alone in my old age! Well, not really old, now, am I, Hunky? I'm in the prime of my life!" Auntie Malice clutched the baby to her chest. "And mothering will be my finest role ever! I shall spank him every day like a good mother should! It tenderizes the meat!"

"Oh, Malice! You idiot! You don't know the first thing about children!" Mama kicked Auntie in the shin. "Now, the first thing is to name a baby."

"How about Pukey?" Auntie suggested.

"Too feminine," my mother pointed out.

"Tsk. That's a shame," Auntie sighed. "He looks like a Pukey. Are you sure he's a boy? Why, of course he is, how silly of me! He's bald! I know, I know, focus, focus, it's just so overwhelming! How about Overcooked Oatmeal?"

"The world and his wife is named Overcooked Oatmeal

these days, Malice. You might as well name him Parking Ticket."

"Well, I don't know what to name *it!*" Auntie was so exasperated she nearly tossed my new cousin off her lap. "I don't see why we have to name it anything at all!"

"How about Bamboozle? That's a nice, respectable, old-fashioned name," sighed Mama, taking the baby from Auntie's arms.

"Ugh, that thing is heavy." Auntie rubbed her biceps. "You've got to help me," she begged.

"I won't," Mama snapped. "This is entirely your problem. Anyway, what am I supposed to do? You can't move in. This cave isn't big enough."

"Hunky can build an addition. Can't you, Hunky? Something dark, out of fudge. You can do it, Hunky, you're a whiz. And Hunky can help you out while I'm out at the soirées . . ."

"What do you mean, *while you're out?*" Mama howled.

Auntie's face got very flat. "Excuse me. I seem to have mistaken you for family."

"You are a manipulative, demanding, unfair *witch!*" Mama went soprano.

"Thank you," said Auntie Malice, calling her broom to

her and moving toward the doorway. "I'll be back in a few days. I need to read up on this. Maybe I'll stop at the spa, get a guacamole facial, too—to bring out the green. I don't want to be one of those mothers who just lets themselves go, darlings," she called to us as she rose higher and higher in the air. "I'll pick you up some dolls from Bora-Bora! And I'll fax you some lullabies! I'm sure I'm just *great* at writing lullabies!"

"Well, this is just dandy," said Mama, when Auntie was no bigger than the size of a black wasp in the sky. "Stuck with a backstabbing daughter and a bouncing bundle of brat."

"I'll make you a carriage house out of fudge," I offered weakly.

"It's the least you can do, isn't it?" she snapped. "Abandoning your own mother like that." I almost reminded her that she threw me out, but it didn't seem like the best time to mention it. "You know, Hunky Dory, when somebody leaves, the whole world changes."

"Not the whole world." I rolled my eyes.

"Yes, the whole world! You listen to me, for a refreshing change." She pointed her knobby finger at me with her free hand. "You can cut holes in things, you careless girl. Your life was different? Congratulations. So was mine. You left an empty space, a vacuum." I looked around, and she was right. The cave looked so empty. Where were all the dolls? Had it been too painful for her to see little witches all around? "After you left, nothing tasted the same. The world seemed painted with dishwater. Your life was fresh and new and full of possibility, wasn't it, because you knew you still had a chance to matter."

"How do you know I mattered?" I accused. "For all you knew, I had been devoured by wolves."

"Btthllp!" Mama blew a raspberry in fury. "Did you think I didn't check how you were doing every single day in my crystal ball?"

"Btthllp!" said the baby.

"You're a know-it-all!
From the tip of your hat to the toes of your cat,
You're a know-it-all!
It seems my life experience
Underqualifies me
For giving you advice, my dear,
It simply mystifies me!
You're a know-it-all!

There's nothing I can tell you
That you don't claim that you knew three days ago!
You ask what you can do,
And all I ask from you
Is to admit there's something your poor old mother
  might know!
You say that I don't love you as you are. Well, I do!
You *think* that I can't learn to understand.
And though I must admit that some decisions you
  have made
Have veered you from the path that I had planned;
I thought you'd be the wickedest witch wherever the
  four winds blow.
I thought you were the best. Was that so wrong?
But now you've got the freshest mouth
Of east or west or north or south,
And so I am compelled to sing this song!

"You're a know-it-all!
I know it hurts to hear
That you're a know-it-all.
Did you know that all along I've been wishing you
  well?
It may sound like heresy,

162

But even as a fairy, see
That once upon a time I was your age,
With dreams and wishes of my own.
And though you consider yourself a sage,
A bit of bitter herb qualifies me for the throne.
You're a know-it-all!
It's a shame that such a sweet little girl should grow
Into an aleck that is smart.
But please, Hunky, have a heart,
And leave a little bit for the rest of us slobs to know."

"I'm sorry," is all I could think to say. "I'll try to be more of a know-it-*some*."

"Don't apologize." She grew aloof. "You see, sometimes 'when you do what you have to do, it helps other people do what they have to do.' *Be the One with the Wand*, chapter ten." She couldn't help laughing a little. "In your absence, I have started a museum."

"What!"

"Just a little museum," she said. "A doll museum. I put the dolls in displays," she explained. "I had an addition put on the back of the cave." She led me through the kitchen to a dark hall, where at least a dozen dioramas were backlit in the cavern walls. I peered into a box. There was Marie Laveau, poling through a Southern swamp while the eyes of a hungry alligator just barely peered out from a polyurethane pool. There was Heckedy Peg at a table with electric candlelight flickering, leaning over to feast before she hears the knock on the door that will end her little party. And my Befana, dragging her sack across the glittery snow in her orange cloak, with one star shining in the midnight blue of the East. "All the little witches like to come and look. Goldilocks brings her friends. And the schedule's very flexible."

I looked at Mama. It was so nice to see the familiar creases in her face. It was even nicer seeing them ironed out a bit. She was glowing. It occurred to me that maybe Mama wasn't so bad at granting wishes, not even her own, when she had to.

"I'm so proud of you," I told her.

"Proud of me! Who is the mother and who is the daughter? Which witch is which?" She smacked me in the head. But not hard—she had the baby. She sighed a tired sigh. "I can't believe it. You know, I was just wishing I would be an aunt. I must have forgotten that I was talking about your Auntie Malice. Now I'm the one laid low by the One-Handed Jinx!"

I took the baby at last, all squishy like a marshmallow. Even Lemon Droppings won't be able to resist this one, I thought.

"Mama," I said. "Do you need help? A gift shop? A café?"

She didn't say anything.

"How about the baby?"

"Don't overextend yourself."

"I can move back."

"You love your house."

I stopped. She was right. I do love my house.

She sighed. "Do you know what you can do for me?" I straightened. "Try to think of a prank to play on your Auntie Malice. You can do that much without a degree from charm school, can't you?"

"Your wish is my command." I smiled gratefully.

She walked away, but turned back. She didn't give me a clock on the head or a pinch on the arm. She bent close to my face. "You'll be the most wonderful F.G. wherever the four winds blow," she whispered. "And you are already the wickedest daughter." I closed my eyes and felt the words fly through me, wild and joyful, like a bat.

"Thhhlllp," the baby blew another raspberry, enjoying his new trick, and looked up at me with eyes the color of autumn. "You're a very clever, clever boy, aren't you?" He

seemed impressed by the fact that I knew how to talk, and watched my mouth with great interest before making a grab for my nose. "Ah-ah-ah!" I chided him. "I'm your cousin, Hunky Dory. I'm your fairy godmother and you have entered a long line of powerful and amazing witches and warlocks. And if you behave, I'll give you a gift." He made a small gurgle, watching and waiting for our first collaboration. I felt the warm, carbonated feeling start to rise from my toes.

"Conflict," I whispered into his ear. "In small doses."

After all, it builds character.

And I can't imagine a better thing to have.

Wisdom from
BE THE ONE WITH THE WAND

- Praise is no substitute for achievement.
- Mimicry is basic to witches and all other brands of bullies.
- Be open to changes.
- Live as though your fondest wish has already been granted.
- Fake it till you make it.
- Don't be meaner than you have to be.
- There's more to you than the job you do.
- Don't work for other people when you can work for yourself.
- There's no voice on the outside that can tell you more than the voice on the inside.
- If you're between a rock and a hard place, stand still.
- Don't open your umbrella before it starts to rain.
- The first step in accomplishing amazing things is setting unrealistic goals.
- Starting over is still easier than going down the wrong path.
- Where you devote your energy, so shall you improve.
- When you do what you have to do, it helps other people do what they have to do.

Hunky Dory's Booger Cookies

INGREDIENTS

Cookie:

1/3 cup powdered sugar

1 cup margarine or butter, softened

1 tsp. vanilla extract

3/4 tsp. almond extract

Small package of instant pistachio pudding

1 egg

2 cups of unbleached flour

1/2 cup chocolate chips

Eye of newt, tongue of frog to taste (optional)

Filling:

1 1/2 cups powdered sugar

1 tsp. vanilla extract

1 to 3 Tbsp. milk

3 to 5 drops green food dye

Witch's hats:

Bag of Hershey's chocolate kisses (dark chocolate if you are really evil)

DIRECTIONS

Preheat oven to 350 degrees.

In a large bowl, cream 1/3 cup powdered sugar, 1 cup of butter, 1 teaspoon of vanilla, and the almond extract, pudding mix, and egg in your cauldron until well blended. Lightly spoon flour into the measuring cup. By hand, bit by bit, stir in the flour and 1/2 cup of chocolate chips until well blended. Chant your favorite spell or sing one of Auntie Malice's hits while you stir; it makes the time pass more quickly.

Shape into 1-inch balls, and roll in eye of newt (pecans or walnuts also work nicely, if you like them). Place 2 inches apart on lightly greased cookie sheet. With thumb or wand, make imprint in center of each cookie. Bake for 10 to 14 minutes until edges are light brown. Let cool completely.

In a smaller cauldron, combine all filling ingredients until smooth, and place a very scant teaspoon of this filling onto the center of each cookie. Top with a witch's hat.

Serves one coven.

Miss Harbinger's Magical Must-Read List for Witches (and maybe even Fairy Godmothers) in Training

Bed-Knob and Broomstick by Mary Norton, illustrated by Erik Blegvad

The Christmas Witch by Ilse Plume

Curse in Reverse by Tom Coppinger, illustrated by Dirk Zimmer

The Dream Stealer by Gregory Maguire, illustrated by Diana Bryan

Glenda Glinka: Witch-At-Large by Janice May Udry,
     illustrated by Marc Simont

Half-Magic by Edward Eager

Harry Potter and the Sorcerer's Stone by J.K. Rowling

A Hat Full of Sky by Terry Pratchett

Heckedy Peg by Audrey Wood, illustrated by Don Wood

I Am Morgan Le Fay: A Tale from Camelot by Nancy Springer

Joan of Arc by Josephine Poole, illustrated by Angela Barrett

Kiki's Delivery Service by Eiko Kadono, illustrated by Akiko Hayashi

The Lion, the Witch and the Wardrobe by C.S. Lewis

Not Just a Witch by Eva Ibbotson

Strega Nona by Tomie DePaola

The Trouble with Miss Switch by Barbara Brooks Wallace

Voodoo Queen: The Spirited Lives of Marie Laveau by Martha Ward

Well-Wished by Franny Billingsley

William Shakespeare's A Midsummer Night's Dream by Bruce Coville,
     illustrated by Dennis Nolan

The Wish Giver by Bill Brittain

The Witch Family by Eleanor Estes

Witches and Witch-Hunts: A History of Persecution by Milton Meltzer

The Witches of Worm by Zilpha Keatley Snyder

Witch Twins by Adele Griffin

The Worst Witch by Jill Murphy